# THE
# China
# TATE
# SERIES

## THE
## ICE
## QUEEN

# LISSA HALLS
# JOHNSON

PUBLISHING

Colorado Springs, Colorado

*For my precious daughter Stacie.*
*Thank you for your ideas,*
*your enthusiasm, and especially,*
*your hugs.*

THE ICE QUEEN

Copyright © 1996 by Lissa Halls Johnson.
All rights reserved. International copyright secured.

**Library of Congress Cataloging-in-Publication Data**
Johnson, Lissa Halls, 1955–
    The Ice Queen/ Lissa Halls Johnson.
       p.     cm. — (Book . . . in the China Tate series ; #6)
    Summary: While serving as a camp counselor for ten-year-old
girls, China wishes she could teach the Ice Queen a lesson but
ends up learning one herself.
    ISBN 1-56179-477-5
    [1. Camps—Fiction.    2. Christian life—Fiction.]  I. Title.
II. Series: Johnson, Lissa Halls, 1955–  China Tate series ; 6.
PZ7.J63253Ic   1996
[Fic]—dc20
                                      96-7475
                                         CIP
                                          AC

Published by Focus on the Family Publishing,
Colorado Springs, Colorado 80995.
Distributed in the U.S.A. and Canada by Word Books, Dallas, Texas.

No part of this publication may be reproduced, stored in a
retrieval system, or transmitted in any form or by any means—
electronic, mechanical, photocopy, recording, or otherwise—
without prior permission of the publisher.

This is a work of fiction, and any resemblance between the
characters in this book and real persons is coincidental.

Cover Design: Jim Lebbad
Cover Illustration: Paul Casale

Printed in the United States of America
96 97 98 99 00/10 9 8 7 6 5 4 3 2 1

# CHAPTER ONE

CHINA JASMINE TATE SAT on the edge of her best friend's bed, a duffel bag on the floor beside her feet. Her bottom lip stuck out in a pout. "I'm going to miss you," she said.

Deedee plowed through a pile of clothes to find her hiking boots. "You're so weird, China."

"So what if I am? Aren't you going to miss me?"

"China, we're going to be one tepee away from each other. You'll be in yours with a bunch of girls, and I'll be in mine with a bunch of girls. We'll eat together, go to campfires together, do crafts together, swim. . . . The possibilities are endless."

"But we won't be sleeping in the same room. I won't have you to look up to in the morning." China loved living with Deedee Kiersey and her family for the summer, even though Deedee's small bedroom had only enough room for one twin bed and a dresser. China didn't mind bedding down in a sleeping bag on the floor.

Deedee tied her boots. "And I won't have you to bounce on my bed in the morning. Or wake me up with your dumb questions."

"I've heard there are *no* dumb questions."

"Whoever said that hasn't met you." Deedee stomped her feet to get them properly settled in her shoes.

"I love you, too."

Deedee swished her hand across the top of China's head. "You're not nervous, are you?"

China kicked her duffel bag. "Of course I'm nervous. I've never been a counselor before."

"We'll go to training this morning and early afternoon. The kids will arrive late this afternoon. By then you'll know so much about how to counsel, you'll be an instant pro. It'll be great."

China wasn't so confident. She'd grown comfortable working with Magda and Rick in the high school camp kitchen. She missed them a lot already, having worked the previous week in the main camp kitchen because a flu bug had zipped through all the regular workers. Now the Tribal Villages needed extra counselors. China didn't much like 10-year-olds. Her younger brother was nine, and he was the biggest pain in the entire world. One year couldn't make that much difference. Now she would be responsible for *five* 10-year-olds for a whole week. Never in all the time since she'd left Guatemala had she felt like going back or going to Aunt Liddy's in Los Angeles. But now her stomach squeezed into a tight knot, and she wondered if she'd rather be in either of those two places instead of an Indian tepee at the other end of Camp Crazy Bear.

Deedee's face came into blurry view two inches from hers. "Yoo-hoo! China! Have I lost you again?"

"Yeah."

Deedee looked closely at China, her eyes narrowing. "Are you okay? Did you catch the flu or something?"

China shook her head.

"Let's go eat breakfast."

"You go. I'll wait here."

Deedee put her hands on her hips. "You always eat breakfast."

"Just go," China said softly.

When Deedee left, China lay back, her hands clasped behind her head. Fear chewed at her insides. It was a different kind of fear from the terror that had run through her when the bears attacked them in the middle of the night. It was a different kind of fear from that sick feeling when she had been locked in the walk-in refrigerator. She just didn't have what it took to lead little kids. She didn't have what it took to lead more than a little dog named Bologna. Even then she messed up.

Mrs. Kiersey stuck her head through the doorway. "Can I come in, China?" she asked.

China nodded and sat up.

Mrs. Kiersey sat on the edge of the bed and leaned

back on her hands. She moved just like Deedee, looked just like Deedee, and talked just like Deedee. China liked her a lot. But she didn't feel like talking to anyone right now.

Mrs. Kiersey put her hand on China's arm. "God never calls you to do something that He doesn't give you the strength to handle, China."

"But how do I know He's called me to this?" China responded. "I didn't hear any voices. I didn't get anything in the mail."

Diana Kiersey chuckled. "And most likely you never will." She smiled just like Deedee. "One thing I've learned many times over, China, is that God expects us to do a whole lot of things by faith. He isn't terribly vocal about what He wants us to do. We have to find the answers in the whispers instead of in big, loud voices or crashes of thunder. We have to want to do things the way God wants us to and then trust that He'll lead us that direction."

China sighed. She flopped down on the bed and rested her chin on her hands. "I don't even like 10-year-olds."

"God will give you the strength—"

"I know, I know."

"But He never promised it would be easy. You never know. Maybe God wants you with these kids to teach you something."

"But what if I mess up? What if I'm the world's worst counselor?"

"If God can work through Peter, He can work through anybody."

"Peter who?" China asked, only half listening. She knew Mrs. Kiersey was sweet, but she was, after all, an adult. Sometimes adults lectured endlessly about stuff that didn't make sense.

"Peter the fisherman. One of the ones Jesus chose to teach His most important spiritual truths to. The one who always put his foot in his mouth. Peter was incredibly opinionated and a little too eager to barge right in and take over."

"Oh, *that* Peter," China said, hoping Mrs. Kiersey would take the hint and end the lecture. Mrs. Kiersey had good points to make, but China didn't know how they would help her feel less fearful of being in charge of five girls she'd never seen before.

"God is bigger than you are, China. Don't ever make the mistake I once did in thinking He's not big enough." She kissed China on the top of her head and stood to leave. "It may or may not make you feel any better, but I'll be praying for you while you're gone."

When she had left, China breathed deeply and prayed, *God, I sure hope You're bigger than a bunch of 10-year-olds all put together.*

Deedee clomped into the room and announced, "Time to go."

"I'd rather die."

"Too bad. That's not on the agenda for the day. You'll have to see if it comes up tomorrow."

China grabbed her duffel and a borrowed sleeping bag. Once she got outside, the mountain air cleared her brain, and her adventurous spirit took over. "Let's imagine . . ."

"No!" Deedee shouted. "I'm not getting into that mess again."

China shook her head. "I learned my lesson. I'm not going to suggest we imagine who and what people are. I just think we should imagine that we're pioneers who've been invited to spend the week with the Indians. We get to see how they live."

Deedee cocked her head and studied her friend. "I don't know. . . ."

"Haven't you ever wanted to travel in time and spend just a little while in another place?"

"Uh, no."

"We could pretend that, too. You and I are somehow caught in a time warp. It's our responsibility to care for these poor Indian orphans. We'll only be there a week, and then we know we can return to our own time."

Deedee's light-colored eyebrows pulled together.

"Come on, Deedee. It'll help me get through this thing."

As Deedee looked up into the sky toward the mountain peaks, a smile came over her face. "Okay. That'll be fun. You could think of it this way, too," Deedee added. "For a whole week, we'll be surrounded by cute guys in Indian outfits."

China's eyebrows raised. "Of course! The other counselors! Well, now, why didn't you point this out before? We could have worked in the village the whole summer. We could be Indian maidens by now. We could—"

"China?"

"Yeah?"

"Promise me one thing."

"What's that?"

"There will be no disasters this week."

"I promise. Trust me."

Deedee cringed. "I hate it when you say that."

After the training meeting, China felt much better about the week ahead. She now had visions of a happy group of girls gathering around her, eager to hear every pearl of wisdom that might drop from her tongue. She pictured their devotions before bed—a holy time when the kids would kneel by their cots and pray to a God they knew they could trust because their counselor had opened windows that allowed them to see Him better. She imagined their lives changed forever because China Jasmine Tate had sacrificed her week for their souls. She pictured fun times of competition and games. They would be excited to join in because, after all, they *were* kids. They weren't stuffy high schoolers afraid to let loose.

She smiled, thinking of the excitement in their eyes.

They would believe this really was an Indian village, where tribes lived in tepees and a chief taught them how to live in harmony with the land and their God.

China linked pinkies with Deedee, squeezing tight. "It's going to be a great week," she said.

Deedee looked at her boots. "I guess so."

"What? I thought you were jazzed about this."

"I was. Until I remembered that it meant I had to go listen to God stuff all week."

"You'll live."

"I don't know. How can I teach the kids all this stuff about God if I'm bored with it? I've heard it all so many times. I'm sure God is there, but I'm not so sure how relevant He is to real life."

"Well, we can be together at the meetings and stuff. I'll help you out as much as I can."

Deedee's smile bordered on falling into a light laugh.

"What?" China asked.

"Here I was supposed to help you make it through the week, and you might have to help me."

"We'll just have to help each other."

## CHAPTER TWO

**C**HINA HATED TO SWEAT. Somehow it didn't seem very attractive or feminine. In spite of her strong beliefs against it, however, the sweat pooled in her armpits and dampened the back of her neck and her forehead. Behind her snaked a long line of soon-to-be counselors, also sweating their way up the mountainside. A couple of grandmotherly types didn't look as if they'd make it up the hill, much less be able to lead and play with a bunch of high-energy girls for a week.

They hadn't been hiking for more than 15 minutes, but it seemed like a long time since China had been able to see any sign of the rest of Camp Crazy Bear. "Are we there yet?" China asked in a little kid's voice.

"You'll know we're there when we've stopped in front of your tepee," a handsome Indian said over his shoulder. China paid little attention to the trail or the weight of her duffel and sleeping bag. The guide, Laughing Squirrel, held all her attention. He wore

Indian-style pants and shirt, along with a necklace made of teeth and feathers. China couldn't help but notice his muscular build.

"He's taken," Deedee hissed into China's ear.

"I can enjoy one of God's marvelous creations, can't I?" China said. "Besides, he winked at me."

"He winks at everyone, China. The guy has a twitch."

After a few more curves in the path, China caught a glimpse of cream-colored objects through the trees. A wooden sign stuck into the ground announced TRIBAL VILLAGE. They walked straight up the hill until they reached a smaller wooden sign. *Cherokee*. Beyond the sign were several picnic tables. Off to one side stood a water trough on legs, with eight water spigots and one water fountain. Small stone-rimmed paths led to four large tepees. Each tepee consisted of a cream-colored, heavy cloth covering with stripes, crude animals, and suns painted on it. Support sticks protruded from the top of each tepee.

China felt mesmerized by how real the tepees looked and how cozy the miniature tribe felt. At the same time, the contrasting picnic tables and water trough made her laugh. "I didn't know Indians ate off picnic tables and had garbage cans," she said to Deedee.

Laughing Squirrel answered, "We have made concessions to the comforts of the white man." He winked. China wondered if that meant he was teasing her or his twitch had overpowered him.

Laughing Squirrel held up his hand to stop the snaking line of counselors. It took a few moments for the stragglers to catch up. In the midst of heavy breathing all around, Laughing Squirrel announced four names. Four college-age guys came forward and were directed to their tepees. "As you enter your tepee," Laughing Squirrel said, "pray for each child in your care for the week—to know how to deal with those young lives. Pray for the counselors in your neighboring tepees. And pray for the safe arrival of those counselors who were unable to come to the training. You are to wait in your tepees until your young Indians arrive."

The guys nodded, grabbed their gear, and moved off to their tepees. China leaned into Deedee. "This is getting far too serious for me," she said.

"Relax. Laughing Squirrel is trying to get everyone into the mood of thinking Indian. It helps the kids create a separate world away from outside influences where they can communicate with God on their own level."

China's eyebrows raised, and she put her hands on her hips. "What? Did you memorize what they said at the meeting?"

Deedee smiled. "I've heard it a thousand times." Then her smile faded. "Just like I've heard everything else."

China had heard Deedee's lament a hundred times, so she'd begun to ignore the past 60 or so. Instead, she felt like skipping up the mountain. This was kind of fun. The village was a little rustic for her tastes, but at least there were flushable toilets in long, low buildings set between every few groups of tents, which Laughing Squirrel called tribes.

The numbers of counselors dwindled as the group moved to each new tribal area. Laughing Squirrel led them around another bend and through a grove of trees into a meadow. Beyond the meadow was a canyon. Off in the distance, China could hear the sound of Grizzly Falls pounding madly on the rocks below. The surrounding mountains stood tall and majestic.

"Wow!" China breathed.

Laughing Squirrel spoke: "Here's your tepee, China." His hand moved out from his body like some Indian game-show host indicating the prize.

Deedee dropped her stuff on the ground. "Great," she said. "Arapaho. This is the best tribe location. We'll be happy here, China."

Laughing Squirrel looked at Deedee and winked. "'We'll be happy?'" he said. "You're up in Cheyenne, Deedee."

China felt the blood drain from her face. "We're supposed to be together," she said quietly.

"No one told me," Laughing Squirrel replied.

"You promised," China said to Deedee, trying to squash the panic rising in her voice.

"I . . . I . . . I . . . just figured . . ." Deedee had a wild look on her own face. Then she fixed her gaze on

Laughing Squirrel and asked, "So can you change it? Switch me with someone else?"

Shaking his head, Laughing Squirrel said, "We have a late-arriving counselor. She will be told to come here to Arapaho." Laughing Squirrel winked. "Besides, we need you in Cheyenne, Deedee."

China looked at the few guys and two girls left in the line behind her. "Who else counsels here?"

"It's going to be cozy. We have a light week, so it will just be the two tepees of girls. You and the other counselor. You can take Rock tepee, and the other counselor will have Water."

China gulped, her mouth drying out quickly. "Who is the other counselor?"

"I don't know her name, but she's a regular at Camp Crazy Bear and is supposed to be quite an expert. I'm sure you two will get along just fine."

Deedee put her hand on the Indian's arm. "Can't I have Sky tepee?" she asked.

Laughing Squirrel shook his head. "We have to spread out the counselors who know Camp Crazy Bear well."

"Can't I trade with the other counselor here? I'm sure she won't mind."

"I'm sorry, Deedee, but we cannot change at this time. The registrar won't know to tell the new counselor." He paused, looking at both girls' stricken faces. "It will be okay. The great God is to be trusted in all things."

With that, he turned and moved up the mountainside. Deedee followed him, walking backward. China watched the small group, now more like a worm than a snake, wind their way up the hill until they disappeared through the trees.

The duffel and sleeping bag suddenly seemed too heavy to carry. As China picked them up and looked around the desolate area, loneliness settled over her. She didn't even feel she could fight it. It overwhelmed her, suffocating her with a heaviness like a wool coat on a summer day. It didn't seem to matter that the view from the picnic tables was magnificent. Listlessly, she went to Rock tepee and dropped her gear on the asphalt floor.

Sitting on the nearest cot, she looked around the tepee and swallowed hard. Her heart raced as she counted the empty cots. There were five of them— five little, flimsy beds on stick legs, waiting for five 10-year-olds to lay their junk on them. *I don't know if I can do this, God,* she prayed silently. *I can't keep my own brother in line; how do I expect to keep five little strangers in line? And without Deedee as my strength . . .*

As soon as the thought popped into her head, she knew what God's answer would be.

*I am your strength.*

China sighed. "Okay, okay. I'll try to deal with it." She stuffed down her fear, hoping God wouldn't notice.

The bed directly opposite the open tepee flap

seemed the most appropriate place for the counselor to sleep. That way she would not only be in the middle of all the girls, but she would also be able to watch the door at all times. Spreading out her sleeping bag, China lay down on her back to pray some more.

*Let's see, God. I'm supposed to talk to You about this week. I'd love for You to do something through me to make a difference in the life of at least one of these girls who are going to be here. I'm really scared of them, but I think maybe we'll have a lot of fun.*

China closed her eyes, trying to block out the fear. Instead, she began to picture all the fun things they could do. Take hikes. Sing before bed. Tell crazy stories. Go on the Blob together. Yeah, the girls would love the Blob, the huge, rainbow-colored inflatable pillow in the lake that campers could play on.

The pictures swirled in her mind, then began to run together. Hiking across the Blob, singing under-water, telling stories . . .

A sound grated across the chalkboard of her sleep. Gritty. Spine-chilling. China's subconscious tried to warn her. Rouse her. And slowly, China responded.

"This *isn't* really happening to me," a voice whined. "It *can't* be. There *must* be some mistake. This isn't what Daddy had in mind. I'm *sure* of it."

China tried to drag herself out of deep sleep but couldn't quite seem to do it. She wasn't sure if she heard a foot stomp in the tepee across the way or if she just imagined it.

"I want out, and I want out *now.*"

"You have agreed to counsel. The need is here," another voice answered.

"I *thought* I was going to counsel high school girls."

"Your age is not enough."

China was beginning to recognize Laughing Squirrel's way of speaking. And the other voice sounded so familiar. . . .

"Well, junior high then."

"You need to be in college to counsel junior high."

"I'm very mature for my age."

"God's wisdom is more than our own. He wants you here for a reason."

"Maybe to torment me. Come on. Just get me out of here."

China moved to the open flap of her tepee and saw Laughing Squirrel leaving Water tepee.

The feminine voice inside changed. It now sounded breathy and full. If the girl's tepee had windows, they would have been steamed up. "Please, Laughing Squirrel. I'll . . ."

"A no does not change, Heather. You are needed. Your knowledge about Camp Crazy Bear will be important to the counselor sharing Arapaho."

The world suddenly dipped out from under China. *No!* she thought. *It can't be true. It can't!*

# CHAPTER THREE

**H**EATHER? *Did he say Heather?*

China moved away from the tepee flap. One needed to see Heather when one was ready. Of course. *That's why the voice sounded so familiar, yet not pleasantly familiar.* China sat on a cot in the curve of the tepee, hidden from Heather's sight. She held her head in her hands. Her thoughts whirled, trying to find something to grasp hold of. She could think of only one thing. *God, do You love to play cruel jokes on me? I'll bet You're up there laughing hysterically.* China figured she'd be laughing hysterically, too, if she could actually breathe.

Those thoughts didn't help her get a grip so she could go out to say hello. How do you say hello to someone who hates you?

As soon as Laughing Squirrel was out of earshot, China could hear the ranting of a crazy person inside Water tepee. "My *stupid* father! I'm going to get him for this! I swear I'm going to get him! He's a liar! A creep!"

17

China found a tiny hole in the side of her tepee. She had to bend over in a scrunched way to see out of it. She pressed her eye to the hole, eager to see what Heather did when she thought she was alone. A sleeping bag flew out of Water tepee, followed by a pillow. Then came a pen and a book of some sort. Then out came Heather herself, wearing a short summer dress.

Heather shook her black hair like an angry horse shaking its mane. "What am I supposed to do now?" she demanded of no one. "Why does everything have to happen to *me?*" She took tiny steps forward, her sandals creating dust clouds with each step. "It's so *dirty* here. How can they expect me to maintain my hygiene habits? Uuuhhh!" She twirled around and disappeared into the darkness of the tepee.

*Heather's got it right, God,* China said silently. *Now what am I supposed to do?* She let out her breath slowly and sank onto the nearest cot. She was so caught up in the horror of sharing a tribe with Heather for a week that she landed a little too hard on the cot. The flimsy bed flipped over, dumping her on the asphalt floor.

"Oomph!" All the air rushed out of China in an ugly grunt.

"What was that?" shrieked Heather. "Who's spying on me?"

There was nowhere to run, nowhere to hide. The tepee looked solid all the way to the ground. China did the next best thing. She picked up the overturned cot, ran to her bed, and flipped open her Bible, pretending to be engrossed in it. She knew when Heather arrived, because all the light went out of the tepee. She assumed her best casual expression as she put her finger on the verse she was "reading" and glanced up. "Why, Heather!" she said. "What a surprise!"

Heather's already stormy face grew darker. "I can't *believe* this!" she said. "You set me up for this, didn't you?" Her voice edged up the decibel scale, sounding something like a building hurricane.

"Heather," China said, talking over Heather's mounting anger, "I had nothing to do with this. Honest."

"You are a liar and a thief, and I don't believe you had nothing to do with this. You have a sick mind."

In the background, new sounds caused China's heart to race even faster. *Zareba Fungoid. They're here.*

Heather stopped mid-shriek, her face blanching. "I gotta get out of here," she breathed, and then she slipped out the door.

Many voices filled the air. Excited voices. Shouting voices. Boys calling to each other, hooting at the girls. Girls shrieking. Another male voice of authority China hadn't heard before. "Those Indians with orange wristbands will stop off at Arapaho. As you already know, wristbands with R will be in Rock tepee. . . ." The Indian guide had hardly finished explaining when the complaints began to pour in and past him as the girls made the final trek to their tepees.

"That means Irene is with us!" moaned one girl.

"Our week is ruined," complained a loud voice. "I might was well go back and stay with my parents."

"Who says we have to be nice to her?"

"Maybe she'll get lost."

"Maybe she'll have a heart attack coming up the hill."

Giggles.

"Look at her way back there. She'll never make it up here."

China's head spun. Too much was happening at once. Heather's livid face, her voice gearing up to a deafening shrill, terrified one part of her. Her campers, with a different kind of shrill voice, terrified another part. She braced herself, glad for the counselor training on how to greet her campers. She hoped it would go just like in the video training film. As the girls marched through the door, she smiled and said in the cheeriest voice she could muster, "Hello! Welcome to Rock tepee in the tribe of Arapaho."

The girls clustered just inside the door. "Are *you* our counselor?" a beautiful African-American girl asked. She took great pains to look China up and down. Her beaded braids clacked with every move. China knew she didn't pass inspection by the look on the girl's face.

"Yes, I am," China said, hoping they couldn't hear the nervousness in her voice. "And we're going to have a *great* week."

"I want this one," the girl said as if China hadn't even spoken. She claimed the cot nearest the door. "If the boys come to raid us, I'll have the best view."

Three other girls dropped their gear onto cots, then dragged the cots all to one side of the tepee. One lone cot remained on the other side. "Can you move your cot?" the outspoken girl asked China. "We'd like to all be together."

China considered this unexpected turn of events. It was obvious these girls intended to live their week as though China and the remaining girl didn't exist. *This week doesn't look good, God,* China said silently. *First Deedee, then Heather, now bossy 10-year-olds.*

All the girls looked at China expectantly. She looked back at a row of fresh-scrubbed faces with perfectly combed hair. "Well?" demanded the girl, seemingly the spokesperson for all.

China smiled. Even though her smile was fake, she figured the girls wouldn't know the difference. They also couldn't know her heart beat like crazy. "No, I don't think so," she responded. "We're going to rearrange the cots the way they were."

The girl glared at her. China smiled back. "Do you need help?" China asked, sounding just like her mother.

"Nooo!" the girl said, the word sliding up and down the musical scale. Reluctantly, all the girls moved their cots back to where they belonged.

*Counselor 1, campers 0.*

As the girls settled in, China watched them, hoping God would give her a sign indicating which camper He wanted her to focus on—which girl's life would be changed because China was there. She wanted to know early in the week so she could focus on that girl and pour herself into her. But God didn't give her a clue. *You never make things easy, do You, God?*

"Okay, girls," China chirped. "As soon as the other girl arrives, we're going to have a little get-acquainted time."

"But we already know each other," whined a small girl who looked Vietnamese.

"Here comes Irene," muttered a strawberry-blonde.

For a split second, China wondered how this girl could know someone else was coming. China heard nothing. Then came the smell . . . a potent, preadoles-cent-unwashed-body smell mixed with the odor of a locker room.

When China saw the girl who was her last camper, she almost turned her head away. Irene was very round and short and painful to look at. She had a wide, bulbous nose, tiny eyes set lopsided into her puffy face, and lips so full you could almost swear someone had punched her and caused swelling.

Her hair looked like something China's grand-mother had worn in her high school pictures. China did some quick math and figured it was a style that must have been popular more than 50 years ago—short, black, curly, but clinging closely to her head.

Sweat poured off the girl. Her clothes had dark blue wet spots going from her armpits down to her thick waist. To top it all, she wore a dress—not any old dress, but one so old-fashioned that it would have taken her grandmother down Memory Lane. Coming from a missionary family that didn't have much money, China knew what it was like to wear outdated, less-than-trendy clothes . . . but not like this girl wore.

The other campers had all suddenly found reasons to be busy. They would have run outside, but China blocked the door.

"Hi," China said to the newcomer, "I'm China."

The girl stared at her without expression.

China noticed that the girl was wearing the pointiest and stiffest-looking bra she'd ever seen. Finally, China asked, "What's your name?"

The girl stared at China some more, then looked as though she might be thinking. "Irene," she finally said.

"Nice to meet you, Irene."

The girl stared blankly.

"Why don't you put your things on the cot right here, next to mine."

Irene stared in the direction China was pointing as if she weren't quite sure which cot was the empty one. Then she moved her bulk slowly to the bed.

"She is *so* stupid!" whispered one of the girls loud enough for the whole tepee to hear.

"Okay, girls, we're going to sit in a circle, Indian-style, and get to know each other," China said. Silently she prayed, *Well, God, it seems obvious Irene is the one You plan to change with my presence as a counselor. Please help me. It's going to be tougher than I thought.*

The girls moved as if they were used to being herded from one place to another. They did it smoothly and efficiently.

"This week we're going to be a new family," China began.

One girl looked pointedly at Irene and said, "Gross."

China frowned at her without stopping her little speech. "We're going to do everything together—eat, sleep, play, hike, study the Word of God. Since we're a new family, we need to get to know each other." China paused, then spoke before the African-American girl could say anything. "I know you all know each other, but I don't know you. So this is more for me than for you. I want each of you to tell me your name and then one of your most embarrassing moments.

"I'll start. My name is China Jasmine Tate. My most embarrassing moment was . . . " China blushed. She had so many, it was hard to decide which one to use. And so many of them she couldn't share with these kids. Then she figured she'd tell them a safe one.

"When I was a little kid, I went to the grocery store with my mom one day. A Popsicle had melted in the freezer case, then refroze. When my mom wasn't looking, I leaned in and tried to lick up the gooey stuff. But my tongue stuck to the metal shelf. I stayed stuck until they got some warm water to unstick it. Some kids from my school came by and laughed at me. By the next day, the whole school knew about it."

The girls all laughed—all except Irene. She sat in a rumpled lump, staring into space.

"My name is Lana," the strawberry-blonde said. She was so tiny, it didn't seem she could possibly be 10 years old. "I was running through school to get to lunch one day when I slipped and fell down the stairs, landing at the bottom with my legs all stuck out. Of course that was picture day, and I had worn a dress to school."

The Vietnamese girl spoke next. "I'm Li, and when I was new to this country, I went into the men's rest room, and all these men lined up against the wall turned their heads to look at me. I was so embarrassed. I ran out and started to cry."

"Mine's the absolute worst," the black girl insisted. "At recess one time, we were all standing around talking about stuff, and I started talking about a girl, telling everyone how ugly and stupid she was, and her cousin was one of the people I was talking to."

China raised her eyebrows but said nothing.

Li poked the black girl and said, "Your name, Mashiek. You're supposed to tell her your name."

"Oh, yeah. I'm Mashiek." She flashed a smile that would light up the darkness. China decided she couldn't be all bad.

China looked to the next girl, a quiet one of no

outstanding qualities. She wasn't pretty. She wasn't ugly. She wasn't fat. She wasn't thin. She was the tallest of the group. Her hair was a brown like so many other brown-haired girls. She wore a wide headband on top of her straight hair.

"I'm Melody," the girl said in a quiet voice. "I got permission to go to the bathroom during class one day. When I came back, the whole class started laughing at me. I had a long piece of toilet paper stuck in my shoe." She told her story without the dramatics the other girls had used to tell theirs. She blushed thoroughly when she was done.

"Irene?" China said to the last girl. "What was your most embarrassing moment?"

Irene looked up from her lap and stared at China. China waited for what seemed like an eternity. "Do you have an embarrassing moment?" China asked. Then she smiled, hoping that would encourage her.

Irene licked her oversized lips before she answered, "No."

China prayed quickly, *This is going to be a lot harder than I thought, God.*

## CHAPTER FOUR

**T**HE GIRLS IMMEDIATELY took to their new home, sweeping out the tepee with gusto, then lining the path to their door with small, round rocks they found about the camp. When dinner came, they were one big, happy family—with the exception of Irene.

China didn't know what to do with Irene. She wanted to give her an immediate bath. It was difficult not to gasp for air after an hour in a hot tepee with her. China hated herself for wishing Irene had ended up in another tepee, so she tried to get her involved in the dinner conversation. But the talk usually changed to a different subject with lightning speed, while Irene was still trying to decide whether to serve herself some peas.

The girls at the Rock tepee dinner table had obviously decided to enjoy themselves and pretend Irene wasn't there, fouling the smell of buffalo wings. They clustered together on the uphill end of the picnic table, while China felt obligated to keep Irene company on the downhill end. China smiled at Irene frequently, while Irene returned the smiles with blank looks.

Heather's group from Water tepee had chosen the picnic table farthest from Rock's table. Mashiek had noted their isolation with a loud "Hmmph."

"Probably because of Irene," Mashiek announced. "They want to eat a nice dinner. Why can't we?" She directed her question at China.

"It's not because of Irene," China whispered, looking out the corner of her eye at Heather. Heather had twisted her body so that her back, not her face, would be seen by Rock's table. Her voice had taken on that tone of haughty superiority China had learned to hate. Because of the constant, quick conversation at her own table, China couldn't hear exactly what Heather said. Whatever it was, her girls were glued to every word that dripped from her lipsticked mouth. Her manicured hands moved as gracefully as a dancer's.

China had hoped crazy stuff would hold off for one week—that for just one week she could be a semi-normal person to whom bizarre stuff did not happen. But no. It seemed as if someone, somewhere, was waiting for a thought to cross China's little brain— any thought that could be twisted into something quite unlike what she intended. And then—*whammo!*—it would strike.

Before she could stop it, one of those thoughts came whistling through her head. The moment it flashed by, she knew she was in for big trouble. *I only hope nothing happens in front of Heather,* her thought said to her.

One by one, the girls got up from their places to go say hello to their friends at Water table. Only Irene and China were left. China was distracted by taking a bite of chicken or she would have seen it coming. The hill . . . the unbalanced picnic table . . . the large Irene. The table tilted, and plates, cups of punch, silverware, China, and her chicken bone—all landed in a heap on the dusty ground. Irene's dress hiked up her chubby thighs and came close to revealing her underclothes.

Mocking laughter rained heavily around them.

"I'll bet this is your most embarrassing moment," China said to Irene, shoving three plates off her lap.

Irene looked at her, at the picnic table seat still pinned beneath her, and back to China. "No, it isn't," she said in her plain voice. "This happens all the time."

China wasn't sure her tailbone would ever be the same. She knew her pride wouldn't. Nor would her authority as great and mighty counselor, especially since Heather was saying in her quietly ruthless tone, "This, young ladies, is not the kind of behavior you ever want to take part in."

China put the chicken bone in her mouth and bit down hard so she wouldn't say a word. She got to her knees and began to pick up the mess around her. After a minute, she took the bone from her mouth and instructed, "Come on, girls. Come help. These are your dinner plates."

The laughter ceased, but not because of China's order. A shadow crossed the upturned table.

"Wow," Mashiek said softly, her eyes wide and full of admiration.

"She is prettier than anyone in the whole world," sighed Li.

Heather turned and gave Li a quick, sweeping look, her expression condemning the traitor. Only Irene seemed oblivious to the beautiful Indian woman standing in front of them. China sat back on the ground. She figured this woman was for real, not just a college kid with an Indian name slapped on for the summer. The woman's thick, long, black hair looked purple in the sun. A beaded headband crossed her perfect brow. Her soft leather dress had beaded decorations sewn onto it. Moccasins covered her slender feet.

"I am Singing Bird," the woman said in a voice filled with quiet strength and a hint of why she had been given her name. "I am your tribal chief. I will be your guide, your leader, your helper for the week. If you have any needs, please come to me."

She looked at the mess on the ground. "We will not use this table anymore this week. Come, girls. Let us help our sisters."

Mashiek and Li practically flew to China's aid. They smiled at Singing Bird every possible moment. Melody and Lana helped set up the cleaning station. Irene sat in the dirt and finished her dinner, even though the dirt had turned to mud on her punch-drenched hands.

After dinner and cleanup, China discovered fat mosquitoes liked the Tribal Villages. So did the bees. So did the little clouds of gnats that swarmed in the shade. China pretty much ignored the bugs, and the bees were more of a nuisance than a threat. She really disliked getting gnats up her nose, in her eyes, and down her windpipe. But what she hated the most were the bathrooms. They looked normal enough from the outside: long, low cement-block buildings with GIRLS written on one opening and BOYS on the other. But inside, the awful truth was more than she could take. There were no ceilings on the buildings and no doors on the stalls.

After her unpleasant trip to the bathroom, China had her girls gather their Bibles for the evening meeting called the council fire. China couldn't be happier that Singing Bird took the leader's role, walking them as quiet, respectful Indians to the rough amphitheater carved out of the mountainside. China felt more like a klutzy, failing counselor than a leader. She wasn't even sure she had enough confidence to read the small map they had given her at the counselors' meeting earlier.

Heather's girls could have been mistaken for either proud Indians or haughty kids. They walked like little clones of Heather—with their heads up, their bodies erect, and a definite swish to their walking motion. China's girls walked well behind China. She had put Irene directly behind her, and the other girls didn't want to be anywhere near Irene. Singing Bird had to speak sternly before Mashiek moved her group closer.

China could have danced for joy when she discovered Deedee's campers were to sit right next to hers. China rolled her eyes and leaned into her friend. "You wouldn't believe . . ."

But Deedee obviously wasn't listening. Instead, her eyes widened as she stared at the other group of little Indians. "Heather?" she said, her voice at once a question and an incredulous statement. "What's she doing here?"

"She's the other counselor in Arapaho."

"No!" Deedee turned, still wide-eyed, to look at China. "And she hasn't killed you yet?"

"Thanks a lot."

Deedee shook her head. "This isn't going to be the week I thought it was going to be."

"No kidding."

"I'm really scared, China."

"Why?"

"I've got nothing to give these kids. Nothing."

The kids Deedee could do nothing for were clustered around her as though she were their mother hen. One leaned on her while Deedee absently played with her hair.

"I tell you, China, I'm supposed to be this wonderful Christian answer machine, and I can't do it."

The beat of the council drum demanded the Indians become silent immediately. Laughing Squirrel had the kids singing in no time. Unlike the high school kids who took a couple days to warm up to the songs, these kids sang their hearts out right away. Deedee's tepee won the coup stick for the best singing. The girls sat proudly, a feather-and-leather-decorated stick jutting out of the ground next to them.

After the songs, Laughing Squirrel and the other tribal chiefs put on skits to set out the rules for the kids. No boys in the girls' tribes, and no girls in the boys' tribes. No candy or food allowed in the tepees. Buddy system at all times. Shoes on at all times.

It amazed China to see how they could get the rules across without just listing them in a way that would have bored everyone. Instead, they had the kids and counselors laughing.

More songs followed the skits, and then came the council talk. The great God of this village had a message to bring to them. It was such an important message that it must be given in five parts. The first part would be tonight, told through the great Indian chief himself, Chief Black Bear.

China shivered at the mention of a black bear. She and Deedee linked pinkies and hoped no one would notice. China would miss giving her talk on black bears to the campers this week. She hoped nothing bad would happen without it.

The message from the great God had to do with the things He had made—the world, the trees, the rivers, the animals. All things made by Him were precious, just like the items made by children for their parents. All must be treated with respect. "Respect does not mean placing them at a higher level than man," the chief said. "But it also means we must not treat them poorly, as though they have no value."

The more the chief spoke, the more China could see God growing bigger and bigger. He wasn't so small that He only answered prayers if you prayed them a certain way. He wasn't so small that He could only help people with big problems.

As the night grew darker, China felt herself grow smaller and smaller thinking about a God so big that the universe was a small thing to Him.

The single-file walk back to the Arapaho tribe was almost silent. The girls looked at the sky and into the trees, their mouths open with awe at how big it all was.

Singing Bird's hands fluttered as she spoke. "In 40 minutes, you will hear the song of sleep. When you hear it, all flashlights must be turned off and all voices made silent. In the morning, you will wake to three beats of the village drum."

In her tepee, China felt overwhelmed by the responsibility given to her. Five lives to guide. At the counselors' meeting, they had said so much about the importance of a week at camp in a child's *entire* life. It was more responsibility than China cared to have. She could only hope that the giant God who cared about tiny details would care enough about her kids to speak to them in spite of her weaknesses.

China tried not to be embarrassed about the obvious differences between her body and those of her little campers. But as she changed her clothes, all eyes except Irene's were on her. Quickly putting on her T-shirt and boxers for bed, she slipped outside to look at the magnificent world beyond. She walked behind the tepee, her footsteps silent, and sat on the cool meadow grass, holding her knees close to her chest. She took in the depths of the canyon and let her mind and vision move up the sides of the mountain to the stars beyond.

"I'm not staying."

The voice jarred China's prayerful reverie. No one answered Heather's statement.

"You can't make me."

Silence.

"I want to go *now.*"

"The God who is great can do something great even here with you this week," Singing Bird told her.

"Don't give me this God stuff for an answer."

"But when it is the true answer, how can I give another?"

Now it was Heather's turn to be silent.

"If you wish to leave, where will your children go? We do not have enough room for them. They will have

to go home. I wish that you stay, that you see how big
God can be."

"But what about that other counselor masquer-
ading as a human being?" Heather said, venom spew-
ing from her voice. "Why do I have to share a tribe
with her?"

"God is even so great that He can heal this divi-
sion."

"You guys are hopeless," Heather said.

Something in her voice made China want to raise
her eyebrows. *Heather backing down?* This was new.
China moved back into her tepee and gathered her
pajama-clad girls in a circle. She opened her Bible,
asking Mashiek to hold the flashlight while she read
to them from Job 38. Chief Black Bear had asked all
the counselors to open the Book with the greatest
truth and wisdom and read to the young Indians
about how great this God must be.

When China finished, the first strains of Singing
Bird's soothing voice began the Indian Lullaby. The
song made China cry as she fell asleep.

# CHAPTER FIVE

"**O**H, GROSS!" Mashiek dipped a spoon into drippy scrambled eggs. "Don't they know we can get poisoned from this stuff?"

China slipped into her mother-hen mode. "If you don't like them, eat something else. Have some sausage."

"I can't eat pork."

"Have some cereal."

"It has too much sugar."

"Starve then."

Mashiek grinned, ladled two heaping spoonfuls of limp hash browns onto her plate, and topped them off with three pieces of soggy buttered toast.

China herded her other girls through the chow line, then went back to the tepee to look for Irene. She found her sitting on her cot, staring somewhere beyond her shoes she had put on the wrong feet.

"Are you coming out to eat, Irene?" China asked.

"Yeah," she said without looking up.

"They keep our schedule tight. We're going to have to eat quickly."

"Yeah." Irene still didn't move.

China went to her and reached out a hand. "Come on."

Irene looked up. "Can't," she said.

"Why not?" China was ready to scream. She never knew slow people could make her so crazy. *I guess I've never been around a slow person before,* she thought.

"Can't zip my dress."

"Want me to help?"

"Yeah."

China got Irene to stand and turn around. After zipping, they walked to the chow line. Nothing was left except runny eggs and Mueslix cereal. Half-eaten bowls of Lucky Charms, Apple Cinnamon Cheerios, and Trix swimming in milk sat around. Irene helped herself to a plateful of eggs and three bowls of cereal. China took one bowl of cereal and three packets of sugar. She wanted desperately to ask her girls if she could finish their pieces of toast that already had half-moon bites taken out of them.

The Water tepee occupants sat prim and proper at their table. Every girl had her eyes glued to Heather and how she held her silverware, how she moved, and how she combed her hair out of her eyes with her fingers. Each time Heather moved, they all moved in unison.

"She is *so* pretty," Li whispered to Lana. "I wish I could be in her tepee."

"Pretty isn't everything," China said, pretending her feelings weren't hurt. "It's what's inside that counts." She wasn't really convinced herself.

"Naw-uh," Mashiek said, shaking her head violently, braids snapping in the air. "No boy looks at a girl who isn't pretty. And we all know it's guys that count."

"Maybe a boy isn't worth it if he only cares about how a girl looks," China protested.

The girls all looked at each other as if this were a completely new concept. Then they shook their heads. "Naw," Mashiek said.

"Boys don't look at me," Irene said.

The girls stared at each other, then burst into laughter.

Singing Bird suddenly appeared. It was as though she never really came and went, but appeared and disappeared. "I am glad we have no spilled tables or girls this morning," she said. China blushed. Irene just sat there, shoveling food into her mouth, barely giving herself time to chew.

"When all is clean, we will have our trail talk."

Heather's hand shot up in the air. "What's that?" she asked.

"A hike during which we learn more about God and His creation."

"I can't hike in this," Heather said, indicating her short dress and flimsy sandals.

"You may change."

"I don't have anything to hike in."

Singing Bird looked her over, then looked at China. "Perhaps China would loan you something of hers that is more appropriate."

Heather's eyes narrowed. She placed her hands on the table, standing to deliver her reply. "I would *never*," Heather sputtered, "wear anything that *slum* child has put on her body."

"Those are not words of kindness," Singing Bird said.

China waited for a smart-aleck comment from Heather, but none came. Maybe that was because Singing Bird had spoken with such authority.

"We will meet, in single file, in five minutes," Singing Bird said.

The girls scrambled to clean up. Heather's girls had to change into hiking clothes. Heather returned wearing spotless white tennis shoes and her dress, muttering about how she had always sworn she would never be caught dead wearing something unfashionable. She glared at China as though the whole thing were her fault.

China figured she should care, but she didn't. Heather no longer scared her. She was a nuisance that needed to be avoided—nothing more.

China had her girls walk directly behind Singing Bird, who taught them how to walk silently. "The careful walk makes it possible for an Indian to respect the habitat of the animals and disturb them as little as possible," she said in her soft, clear voice. "It also helps them to see and experience shy creatures. Walking silently shows respect for God's creation."

The girls giggled and talked while they tried to make silent footsteps. China wondered if all kids were as unclear on the concept as these girls seemed to be.

Singing Bird taught them how to walk safely down a steep mountain, especially one with loose dirt and rock. "Sideways stepping gives you more surface area upon which to support your weight," she said.

After Singing Bird taught the basics of walking, she led them to a tiny clearing where rough-cut logs lay. The girls sat on them to rest, while Singing Bird told them a story of the forest. She spoke of creatures so tiny they couldn't even be seen, and of the majestic grandeur of the mountain. The more she spoke, the more China felt her mind swimming with the amazing reality of the size and abilities of God.

A couple times, she glanced at Heather, who sat ramrod straight, hands folded on her lap. Her face looked toward Singing Bird, but China doubted if she heard anything the Indian woman said.

Irene also seemed to hear nothing. She sat in the dirt, her knees up and spread apart. She held a stick and poked the ground with it. The other girls seemed to enjoy every word Singing Bird spoke. They fidgeted with sticks, rocks, twigs, leaves, shoelaces, and Velcro, but they nodded and smiled and asked good questions, so China knew they listened.

On the way back to the tribe, Singing Bird led them in wild camp songs with big hand motions and skipping, marching, or strutting steps. By the time the girls got back, they were ready for competition. They had a cheer perfected. But most of the noise seemed to come from the Rock tepee group rather than from Water.

The competition was unlike anything China had experienced at the high school camp. The Tribal Village would compete to see who could build the best working fire pit. While Chief Black Bear gave his instructions, Heather sat on her knees, smiling coyly at one of the male counselors. He puffed his chest out in response. His weak jaw suddenly became strong as he jutted it forward. Heather gave a wiggly finger wave and mouthed, "Hi, Michael."

China thought she'd be sick. She turned away, looking at her own girls to calm her stomach. Irene inspected the bottom of her shoes. Apparently, something unpleasant was packed between the ridges. She tried to wiggle her body around enough to get her nose down to her shoes, sniffing the air to decipher what precisely she had stepped in. Mashiek was trying to braid Li's straight, black hair into cornrows. Lana's face was turned toward Heather, which was in the opposite direction of the chief. Melody, at least, appeared to be listening.

"Each tepee will use the fire pit they create to cook their lunch," the chief continued. "If you don't build a working fire pit, you won't be able to eat lunch."

Heather must have been listening from some part of her brain. At that last statement, her whole body went rigid. Her attention snapped from Michael to the chief. "I can't *possibly* build a fire pit," she complained.

The chief smiled at her as he responded, "Then you will not eat lunch."

Heather held up her manicured hands. "My *nails* will break. My *hands* will get dirty. This is completely disgusting and inappropriate."

"This is the Tribal Village. This is how the Native Americans cooked every meal. It builds family and teamwork. Now, let's give it all we've got."

China gathered her girls around Irene, knowing it wouldn't do much good to get Irene moving from her spot. "Okay, girls, here's our chance to win another coup stick. I know we can do it. You guys are good workers."

"How would you know?" Mashiek asked.

"I can see it in your eyes," China said lamely. She moved the conversation forward quickly, hoping to sidetrack the girls. "Okay. Mashiek, Lana, and Li can gather the firewood, Melody can dig the fire pit, and Irene can gather rocks for the border. I'll help Irene. Then we'll all try to start the fire."

The girls popped up and scattered with the other kids in the tribes. "Okay, Irene, let's go," China said, offering her a hand.

Irene had finally dug a hunk of the goo out of her shoe and put it so close to her face to smell it that a glob stuck to the tip of her nose. She looked at China's hand and squiggled herself around to get up without help. Her foot caught on the hem of her dress, and she stumbled a little. With some effort, she righted herself.

"You've got something on your nose," China said.

Irene made a swipe at her nose.

"It's still there," China said.

Irene made a couple more attempts, and China gave up. Then she showed Irene what kinds of rocks they would need, and Irene did a thorough job of finding them. China posted herself at the pit site to supervise the gathering of supplies.

Melody scooped out the fire pit with a flat piece of bark provided by Chief Black Bear. The camp didn't want kids pulling bark off trees every week, so they had gathered some and kept it for campers to use.

The process seemed to be going well until China noticed that every time Irene was around, kids snickered and looked in her direction. China was used to the kids making fun of Irene, but somehow, this was different. The next time Irene waddled over, carrying one round stone in each hand, China checked her nose. The blob was missing. A little farther down, she saw the problem. Irene's very stiff bra had slipped— probably gone askew from when she twisted herself up to check her shoe. One cup was definitely going north, the other south.

"Uh, Irene," China said quietly in her ear. "You are, uh, a little lopsided."

Irene looked down. She poked at the one going way up on her chest and said, "Yeah." Without making any adjustments, she walked away to find more rocks.

"Everybody's laughing at us," Mashiek hissed. "Make her fix it."

"I can't make her," China said.

"Then we won't work," Mashiek said, crossing her arms.

"Yeah," Li said, mimicking Mashiek's defiant stance.

Lana stuck out her chin and lined up with the other two. "We won't even be seen by this campfire," she said.

They started to walk off together when China admitted defeat. "Okay, okay. I'll talk to her," she conceded.

Reluctantly, China found Irene and told her, "The girls are embarrassed about your situation, Irene."

Irene's thick, black brows pulled together. "Huh?" she said.

"You know. You being lopsided. Please fix it. You're distracting the boys."

Irene shrugged and began to push and pull and tug at things.

"You should go to the bathroom to do it," China said.

"You're my buddy. I can't go by myself."

"Mashiek!" China called.

Mashiek trotted over to them. China smiled an obviously fake smile at her and said, "You can buddy with Irene so she can fix her problem."

Mashiek glared at China, then motioned to Irene. "Come on," she demanded.

When they returned, the girls were trying to start the fire. Making a spark with flint was no easy matter. Mashiek watched a moment, looking over her shoulder at something, then watched her group again. "It's really not fair, China," she said.

China flipped her long hair inside the back of her shirt to keep it out of the way. "Hmmm?" she said absently, focusing all her attention on Melody's efforts to make a spark.

"I wish I was in Water tepee. They don't have to do any work."

Without looking up, China said, "They also won't get to eat."

"They're already eating."

"What?" China jumped to her feet. All of Rock tepee's attention was focused on their rivals. Heather sat back, laughing and flirting with Mike. She daintily took a piece of meat he offered her. They sat in front of a roaring fire. Small, foil-wrapped parcels of cobbed corn and potatoes lay in the hot coals around the edges. Heather's girls also ate, some already enjoying a treat of marshmallows roasted on trimmed sticks.

It wasn't until China swallowed that she realized her mouth had been hanging open.

Melody nodded as if she already knew the whole thing. "Heather whimpered enough until a tepee of guys came to her rescue," she explained. "They got both their fires going real fast."

China plopped to the ground. "Well, at least we can be proud we did it ourselves." She took the flint and got a spark on the first strike. *I guess sometimes it pays to be angry,* she told herself.

# CHAPTER SIX

**T**HE AFTERNOON FREE TIME wasn't all China had hoped it would be, but it was fun. Being with Deedee was a relief from the never-ending demands of counselor duties. Hot and sweaty, China's girls hiked up the hill to their tepee. Their hands were sticky from the snowcones and candy they'd scarfed down on the way back to camp. They lined up at the water trough and rinsed off.

Mashiek finished first and marched up to Water tepee. "Hey, you guys!" she called in. "What'd you do all . . ." Her jaw dropped open, and she stepped back dramatically, pointing at the tepee. "Come here! Look!" she yelled.

The little gang of girls ran up to Water tepee and gaped as they looked inside. China knew she'd probably get beheaded by Heather for being nosy, but she couldn't resist. She wiped her wet hands dry on her shorts and walked up to the tepee.

It had been transformed. Where once there was

concrete, now there was a carpet. It was square in a round tepee, but it was a carpet. Each cot had a bright cotton fabric covering the sleeping bag. A small fold-away table with a stool in front sat in the middle. Someone had rigged a lighted mirror by attaching flashlights all the way around. Heather, ignoring the gawkers, was intent on doing a makeover of the last of her campers. Each girl sat on her cot with her hands flat on her thighs as bright red fingernail polish dried. Each had a new hairstyle with bows, barrettes, buns, and bobbie pins.

A TV tray was set to one side of the tepee with an open box of cookies, one of mini-doughnuts, and assorted candy bars perched on top of it. A mosquito net draped across the front of the tepee opening.

"Wow," Melody said, taking it all in. Even Irene responded, nodding her head up and down violently. She licked her lips as she stared at all the goodies overflowing the tiny table.

Heather looked up from her client. "You may all leave now. You've had your look, so go away."

China's formerly happy group walked away morosely. Inside their tepee, they dropped to their drab cots. Depression weighed heavily in the air.

"It's not fair," Lana said.

"I say we go live in their tepee," Li said.

Mashiek glared at China with a mutinous gaze. "Why can't we ever have any fun?" she accused.

"We just did," China protested. "We walked to main

camp, made a craft, ate like pigs, and sang all the way back. What wasn't fun about that?"

From Water tepee, the girls could hear Heather's smooth voice. "Singing Bird taught you how to walk correctly," she said, "but she forgot one thing. You need to swing your hips just right. Do it correctly and you will never be without a boyfriend. Okay, watch me."

"You don't teach us how to make boys like us," Mashiek complained.

"Or let us bring good stuff into here," Irene said.

All the girls stared at Irene in surprise. "The dead speaks," Lana whispered.

"It's against the rules to bring junk food—or any food—into the tepee," China explained. "It attracts bears."

"Oh, and I see lots of bears running into Water tepee," Mashiek said, crossing her arms and throwing China a challenging look.

A drum beat slowly. China felt as if all the air had been sucked out of her. "It's time for the powwow, girls," she said.

They reluctantly left the tepee for the small semi-circle of logs placed under a tree at the edge of the meadow. China watched them go and gratefully went to the swimming pool, where she had planned to meet Deedee. The powwow time was the only break the counselors got from their charges every day. It was only 90 minutes, but they desperately needed it.

For over an hour, China and Deedee swam and talked. It felt so good to China to finally be in the company of someone who liked her. She had never known how draining it could be to spend all her time around people who didn't.

After swimming, they spread out their towels on the hot concrete. China lay on her stomach, the warm air covering her like a blanket. She closed her eyes and willed visions of mad little girls to go away.

"Is it really that bad, China?" Deedee asked.

"Worse. They hate me. Maybe we were all wrong. Maybe God doesn't really want me here. He couldn't want me to be here just to make these girls angry. He couldn't want me to be in a hopeless situation with Heather."

"I don't think we made a mistake." Deedee twisted her thick hair until it coiled against her head. She stuffed the ends inside the coil and lay down.

"So what am I supposed to do?" China asked.

"Just be yourself, China. That's the best way to win them over."

"But they don't like my self. They like a Heather self. They want what I can't give them."

When China returned to her camp, she could see the powwow hadn't changed the mood of her girls at all. In fact, it seemed to have made them worse. No one talked to China during dinner. Instead, they all looked toward Heather's table and let loose with huge sighs. You would have thought they were a bunch of orphans peering through the window of a warm kitchen, well stocked with food, family, and love.

At the evening's council fire, they livened up quite a bit. For some absolutely crazy reason, Heather volunteered for the counselor's competition. China's girls held China's hand up for her, even though she really didn't want to compete. She wanted to hide out, play invisible, and go home. She *didn't* want to be up against Heather in some silly game. Reluctantly, China went forward when Laughing Squirrel chose her.

Eight burlap bags covered big cube shapes. Laughing Squirrel chose four girl counselors and four guy counselors to sit on the cubes. China, fresh from five weeks of knowing Kemper, the high school camp director, was very suspicious about it all. Kemper thought up the most bizarre and gross games for the kids to play, so China didn't trust any Camp Crazy Bear games.

"All you have to do is sit," Laughing Squirrel said with a devious twinkle in his eye. "Really."

China looked at him and then beyond for the syrup, the bucket of mud, the ice water—something that would be dumped on them when they sat. But the council fire didn't have many places to hide things.

"Sit, please," Laughing Squirrel said to the contestants.

Heather flashed Mike her whole-body flirt, then chose a cube next to him. As she sat down, her eyes went wide. "Ohhh!" she screeched.

Mike sat and then immediately jumped up. "You've got the wrong person for this," he insisted.

China sat on the farthest cube. Instantly she felt icy fingers go up her spine, then icy water go down her leg. She sucked in a lot of air. "This is cold!" she yelled.

"Of course it's cold!" Laughing Squirrel said. "Those are blocks of ice! The counselor who sits the longest wins a pizza for his or her tepee, points for his or her tribe, and the title of Ice King or Ice Queen!"

One guy shifted to sit on his hands. Laughing Squirrel shook his head and instructed, "No sitting on hands. Or shoes. Or anything except the burlap. No getting up for even a moment."

China heard Mashiek scream her name. She looked up to see Mashiek and the other girls chanting and rooting her on. China wished she'd thrown on the sweatshirt she'd left behind on her cot.

Laughing Squirrel led the kids in singing a couple songs. Before the songs ended, two guys had quit sitting. China wanted to quit. The cold was beginning to hurt. The pain reminded her of another cold she'd felt—in the walk-in refrigerator. She tried to remind herself that she wasn't locked inside a walk-in. She was outside, voluntarily sitting on a block of ice— well, almost voluntarily.

The grandma counselor slid off her block and walked stiffly back to her kids. They all hugged her. Deedee got her tepee to yell for China. China grinned and tried to hold on inside. Another guy jumped up. A petite counselor, who looked a little blue around the edges, also went back to her tribe. The kids sang two more songs. Heather ignored the songs and continued to flirt with the guy next to her. She didn't seem bothered by the cold at all.

China shivered, and her teeth chattered. She looked at her kids and tried to wave. At the same time, she crossed her leg, and in slow motion, something shifted beneath her. The block of solid ice now had a slippery film of water on it. With her movement, the burlap gave way. In one swift motion, China was on the dirt. The kids laughed a little too hard—all the kids except Rock tepee. China moved back to her group, smiling and laughing at herself. She met a wall of stone-hard faces.

Mashiek crossed her arms and spoke for the rest of the kids: "You can't do anything right."

The crowd erupted into cheers as Heather's flirt-mate moved off his block. Heather sat as though she were having tea in the elegant parlor of someone's mansion.

"Tribal Village, I want to introduce you to your Ice Queen," Laughing Squirrel said. He tried to hold Heather's hand over her head, but she would have nothing to do with that. Instead, she held her hand out straight, looking more as if he were asking her to dance. She slid gracefully off her throne and curt-sied—toward the guys' section.

"The Ice Queen—how appropriate," China whispered to Deedee.

Heather returned as the joyous conqueror to her adoring girls. Mashiek and Li gave China a hard look, then turned away. "I *really* wish we could change tepees," Mashiek said loudly to Li.

Li nodded.

Moments after China's group returned to their tepee, Heather's angry face appeared in their door. "You could have asked if you wanted some," Heather spat. "I really didn't think you'd be so low, China."

"What are you talking about?" China asked.

Heather's eyes narrowed. "You know exactly what I'm talking about." She looked around the darkened tepee. "The rest of you know, don't you?"

Four little heads wagged no. Irene had her socks off and was checking between her toes.

"Hey, fatty," Heather said, staring at Irene. "Did you eat all our stuff?"

China marched over to Heather. "It's not right for you to call any of the girls names," she lectured. "Apologize right now."

"I'm not apologizing. You and your girls are little thieves, and I'm telling my girls not to speak to you again."

China wanted so badly to remind Heather who had been caught lying and stealing earlier in the summer.

She would have if she didn't have five little girls listening. Instead, in a restrained voice, China hissed, "What did we steal, Heather?"

"Our goodies. I saw how jealous your girls looked this afternoon. You didn't have to make such a mess of them in the process, either."

"Show me."

"I don't have to do any such thing."

"Look, Heather, it's only fair. You aren't being fair to my girls by accusing them and then not letting me see what you're talking about."

China followed Heather to Water tepee. Inside, the small table had been tipped over. Crumbs of food littered the floor. Shredded candy wrappers lay strewn about. China went over to the mess and got down on her knees.

"I suppose you're going to accuse me of this?" Heather said.

China just looked at Heather. The question wasn't worth a reply. She asked for and got a flashlight. After searching the ground for a few moments, she said, "Come here. You've had thieves all right, but they weren't the human variety."

"Trying to protect yourself?" Heather said, crossing her arms and sneering at China.

Heather's girls got down on their knees next to China. A pretty girl named Rhonda gently pushed on a couple torn packages. "She's right," Rhonda said. "You can see the scratch marks."

China sat on her haunches. "Raccoons, I'll bet. Messy little critters. You'd probably be best off if you cleaned it up tonight. "

"Get out!" Heather demanded.

Everyone shuffled out without saying a word. That night in the tepee, China's girls would have nothing to do with her Scripture reading on how God is not only big, but He even cares about the little details of life.

"I'll bet the Ice Queen doesn't make her kids listen to boring stuff," Mashiek said to Li.

*The Queen*, China thought. *No matter where she goes, she always manages to earn that title.*

"She thought we stole stuff," Melody said quietly.

"But she's cool," Mashiek said. "She knows when rules are stupid and should be broken. She's generous and gorgeous. She's the perfect counselor." Mashiek looked at China, her eyes revealing disdain.

Irene dug in her ears and inspected the results.

"Make her stop," Lana pleaded. "If you're any kind of counselor at all, make her stop."

"Irene," China said, "please stop digging in your ears. That's really gross for other people to watch."

"Don't look then," Irene said, peering at the results of the latest mining expedition.

*God*, China prayed silently, *this whole thing is falling apart. Can I just give up now?*

# CHAPTER SEVEN

China woke suddenly in the silent morning. Thoughts pestered her until she took out her notebook and began to write:

*I suppose God can sometimes be viewed as a mean, old, nasty ogre. After all, when we want to quit, He doesn't let us. He always wants to stretch us beyond our energy and abilities and show us that He's more capable than we think He is. I hate that about God. I really do. Because then I feel as though I'm in a constant state of misery.*

*When the whole thing is all over, I'm always glad He did push me. I've learned a lesson, and, sigh, He's right again, as usual. But at this moment, I'm not thinking terribly happy thoughts about being pushed and prodded and made to continue on in this miserable state of existence. God, I DON'T WANT TO STRETCH!*

*DO YOU HEAR ME? Sigh. I have a real feeling He's not listening to me.*

China put her pen down and looked around at the sleeping "cherubs." At any minute the drum would beat, and they would all get up to glare at her again. She didn't relish the thought any more than she relished a new day of bathroom humiliations, Heather humiliations, and battles with bugs and dust.

She shifted again on her elbows, shoving the pillow under her chest so she could write.

*God, if You're going to use me to change some girl's life this week, it will be a total miracle. These kids hate me! And why? Because I'm not Heather. And Irene doesn't seem to care about anything one way or the other. At least I'm getting used to her smell.*

Chewing on her pen, China stared at her last sentence. She obliterated it in case the kids found her notebook and snooped in it.

About one minute after the three drumbeats, as her little Indians were just stretching and making waking sounds, a horrible scream from Water tepee split the air. China jumped from her cot, tipping it over in the process. On her way out the door, she ran into two little bodies that had also jumped from their beds.

China covered the ground between the two tepees

in five running steps. She ripped back the mosquito netting. "What's wrong?" she asked. "Heather, are you okay?"

"Get them out of here!" Heather half-groaned, half-shrieked. She pointed toward the overturned TV table. Crumbled and ransacked goodies littered the floor where they'd been left from the night before. But now a new army of invaders feasted off Heather's generosity. Ants. Millions. Bizillions.

"Zareba Fungoid," China muttered. "I've never seen so many ants in my entire life."

It probably wouldn't have been so bad if the ants had simply sneaked in and out the closest opening to the food. Instead, however, they marched through the tepee, making a third of the tepee into their territory. The moving masses marched right over the top of Heather's cot, through her makeup, and down to the scattered candy.

"What a mess," Mashiek said, peering around China.

The other Rock Indians (with the exception of Irene) also took turns looking at the disaster. Most of Heather's girls had charged outside the minute they saw their tepee had been taken over. They stood in the cool morning sun, shivering and quietly observing the disaster of their temporary home.

"Get them out," Heather demanded to China.

China bit her cheeks and swallowed, looking down at the moving ground. She wanted desperately to shriek back at Heather and tell her it was her own fault and she needed to clean it up herself. *God, You really aren't fair,* she prayed. *I know what You want me to do. But why should I always be nice to Heather when she's never nice to me?*

Looking up, she suddenly saw in Heather a scared, ashamed little girl who obviously fought to maintain her self-control. Her face moved in ways that looked to China as if she were trying not to fall apart. She looked as if she might dissolve into tears at any moment. However, feeling sorry for Heather did not play into China's decision. She didn't feel sorry for her in the least. But she did know that the frustrating God she had given her life to gently asked her to show Heather some loving kindness and compassion.

"First let me get my clothes and shoes on. We'll help." To her girls she said, "Come on. We're going to help our sisters clean up."

"It's not our fault," Mashiek protested.

"I hate ants," Li said softly. "They give me the creeps."

Melody put her hand on China's arm. In a voice too quiet for anyone else to hear, she said, "Thanks for following the rules." Then she trotted into the tepee.

Irene had most of her clothes on. China automatically went over and buttoned the back of her dress. As soon as everyone was dressed, China assigned cleaning tasks, much to the protests of her girls. Grudgingly they walked over to Water tepee and helped its occupants roll up the sides of the tepee to have more space to sweep ants and crumbs outside. At first the girls put Irene on the "picking up the chunks" detail, but they had to take her off because she kept eating what she picked up. Rhonda and the other girls in Water tepee sprayed the ants with hairspray and deodorant to try to kill them. They put fingernail-polish remover around the outer edges of the tepee, hoping that would make a border to keep the ants from returning.

The harder the girls worked, the haughtier Heather got. China couldn't figure that one out. The most she could come up with was that when things got close to being perfect again, Heather could return to her old snotty self.

Lights started coming on in China's head. *How awful for her!* If things aren't going right, her whole world falls apart. China chuckled to herself. *If I totally fell apart every time something went wrong, I'd always be miserable. I'm glad I'm not Heather.*

The girls had barely sat down at the picnic tables to eat breakfast when a new Indian walked up to their tribe. She had thick, long, blonde hair and round, blue eyes. Her leather squaw dress fit her snugly over a figure that would rival Heather's. She didn't have the slim, straight Indian maiden look but the healthy Southern California surfer-girl look.

"Hi, I'm Misty Meadow," she said in a perky voice made for calling shots at a beach volleyball game. "Singing Bird is visiting the Medicine Man today and can't be here. So I'm taking her place!"

Misty Meadow looked at the girls, then at her watch. "Wow, you guys are starting late. You should be finishing up by now. Did you oversleep?"

China could feel Heather's eyes on her. She wouldn't tell on Heather—and not because Heather bored holes into China's head. China realized that Heather had reached out to her girls the only way she knew how. She hadn't brought danger to the tribe, just pesky visitors that would probably be back tonight.

"Just slower today," Mashiek said before stuffing a whole pancake into her mouth in one bite.

Misty's table talk and prayer weren't bad. They just didn't follow along the Indian mystique Singing Bird had built.

When the dishes were scraped and stacked, ready for the Smoking Buffalo (a huffing white pickup truck) to come get them and return them to the main camp for washing, the girls lined up for the morning hike.

"We'll be joining the Cheyenne tribe this morning," Misty said. "Their leader is also with the Medicine Man."

*Thank You, God,* China prayed. *One tiny spark of hope in this crazy week.*

Deedee waited at the side of the road with her little clutch of campers clustered around her. Their adoring faces watched every move she made. Deedee's face took on an added sparkle when she saw China. "Am I ever glad to see you," she said in a low voice.

"Ditto," China said.

The campers and counselors were introduced to each other. Corrine, the other counselor at the Cheyenne tribe, looked sturdy and athletic. *Soccer,* China speculated. She had that wild yet controlled look about her. She also looked like someone you wouldn't want to mess with.

When all the girls had lined up, Misty Meadow raised her hand for quiet. "We have a long hike ahead of us," she said. "Today we're scheduled to go on the walk that takes us to the farthest reaches of our boundaries. We've got a lot to talk about and a long way to walk. So I don't want any dawdlers!"

Everyone from Arapaho looked at Irene. The girls from Cheyenne, not used to Irene's odor, wrinkled their noses and tried politely to pinch them or turn aside to keep the smell away. Corrine gave her girls a jab. "So there's an earthy smell in the air," she said. "It smells of hard work and effort. Live with it."

Her girls instantly put their hands down.

Heather seemed more subdued than usual. She kept eyeing Misty, then looking away. But with no males to compete for, she kept her hackles down. Her girls stayed closer to the main group than the day before and listened carefully.

China wanted so badly to talk to Deedee. But they had to stay to the rear of their own campers, walking single file down the narrow trail. China was glad she and Deedee didn't often need to talk out loud. As best friends, they were close enough to decipher looks and hand signals. Heather ignored Deedee. China figured since Heather could no longer use Deedee to get a job at Camp Crazy Bear, she saw no need to talk to her.

As they hiked into new territory, something disturbed China. She kept looking up the mountain but saw nothing. She glanced at Deedee a couple of times and saw her own concern mirrored in Deedee's face. She also caught Deedee looking up the mountain and then checking her watch.

Misty Meadow chirruped her way along the path, telling them stories about the Indians and how they lived. There was a marked difference in Misty's talk and Singing Bird's. Misty obviously knew what she was talking about, but it was just information. Singing Bird gave information she knew from her heart and by experience.

Either Misty didn't hear the rumbling that soon started in the distance or she ignored it. China looked quickly back at Deedee, who had her face tilted up, searching the mountaintops. China's girls stopped their whispering and looked at China. She smiled at them reassuringly but didn't feel the smile in her heart.

Another long, low rumble, almost like a lion's purr, rolled through the canyon and bounced off the canyon walls. China hadn't heard anything like it before.

Misty found the fallen logs in the clearing for this particular hike's resting point. As the girls sat, Misty passed out small boxes of juice from a backpack.

"What was that?" China asked Deedee.

"I'm sure it's thunder," Deedee said, looking puzzled. "But I don't see any clouds."

"I thought I saw some hanging around the peaks."

"I think we're okay," Deedee said without conviction. She moved away from China and touched Misty's arm. She mumbled something, and the two walked away from the group momentarily.

"What was that noise?" Lana asked China.

"I think it was a little thunder from the other side of the mountain."

"I'm scared," Melody said.

China wanted to say something to comfort her. But the words she'd written in her notebook earlier came back to haunt her. Was God going to stretch them all? Right here? Right now?

Misty returned to the circle, looking wide-eyed and pale. Deedee walked behind, looking up the mountain. She looked at her watch, then up at the mountain again.

China tried to look casual as she approached Deedee. "What's the scoop?" she asked.

"We can't get back to camp in time if we have a downpour."

"Why do you think we'll have a downpour? It's probably just a little thunder on the other side of the mountain."

Deedee shook her head and said, "I think we'll be

safest here. We're in a clearing rather than under a bunch of trees."

Heather had walked up behind them, using her new silent Indian walk. "We'll get drenched," she said.

Deedee looked Heather in the eye and said, "You'll dry."

"I don't *want* to get wet," Heather complained.

"You go under a tree and you're lightning bait," Deedee explained. "Which do you want?"

Heather's bottom lip stuck out. She spun around and flounced away.

"We're going to warn the kids," Deedee told China, "then sing some fun songs to help keep the adrenaline in check. Hopefully that will instill a sense of fun rather than fear. You game?"

China nodded. She looked up at the mountaintop one more time. Her heart stopped. Huge, dark clouds spilled into the sky, pushed by some unseen hand. *Oh, God. Help!*

# CHAPTER EIGHT

**M**OMENTS BEFORE THE RAIN started falling, Deedee stood in front of the girls. "Hi, I'm Deedee," she said, "and I've lived my whole life at Camp Crazy Bear." Murmurs traveled through the group. "That means I've seen all sorts of things—different kinds of weather, animals, and so on. So today I'm going to give you a talk right here. Rain is going to start at any minute, and it will probably rain real hard. But that's okay. Who didn't take a shower today?"

The girls all looked at each other, embarrassed to admit they weren't clean. Irene finally raised her hand.

"Come on," Deedee said like the loving big sister she was. Small drops started to fall into the dust around them. "No one takes a shower at the Tribal Village. It cuts into your sleep."

The girls laughed. China shot her hand in the air. "Our tribe didn't have time to shower this morning," she said. "We were too busy..."

Heather glared at her.

China smiled back. " . . . helping our sisters on an important project."

Heather's glare turned into a wide-eyed stare.

All of China's girls raised their hands, then Heather's, most of Corrine's, and some of Deedee's.

The rain started to fall even harder. "So now you get your first shower," Deedee said. "No big deal." She put her hands on her hips and scanned the group before she spoke again. "Now, I'll just bet that most of you sing in the shower when no one's listening."

The girls laughed.

"Since we're going to have this huge shower together," she continued, "we're all going to sing in the shower."

Deedee made sweeping motions with her hands as the rain fell harder. "Come on now, everyone stand. Whoever heard of sitting in the shower?"

The girls jumped to their feet, eager to do whatever Deedee told them.

"How many of you have trees in your shower?"

No one raised a hand.

"I didn't think so. That means you shouldn't have a tree in this shower, either. Stay away from the trees or you won't get clean."

Just then, the clouds opened with a ripping sound. Water poured on them as if someone held buckets over their heads. Some of the girls screamed and ran for cover.

"No!" shouted Deedee over the noise of pounding rain. She shoved her thick hair away from her face. "No trees in the shower!"

Reluctantly, the girls moved back to the group.

Deedee got the girls to huddle together in a circle. First they sang "The House on the Rock." They sang of the rains coming down and the floods coming up, but the house on the rock stood still.

Lightning flashed, illuminating everything with an eerie glow. Deedee put her arms around the girls closest to her and pulled them in. Thunder rocked the ground.

She had them sing a song about Noah. Then they sang about rain and God and trusting Him. With each flash of lightning and crash of thunder, fewer girls screamed. China worried about Irene, who looked a greenish color whenever the lightning shined on her face. She seemed more dazed than usual.

Mashiek, ever the dramatic one, started to scream they were going to die, but China clapped her hand over Mashiek's mouth when all she had gotten out was, "We're gonna . . ." Li cried silent tears while she sang. Lana did what she was told, holding on tightly to Melody's and Li's hands. Melody looked like the rock in the group. She wasn't totally calm, but she didn't look scared to death. She even looked at Irene, forcing out a little smile and squeezing her hand. Irene didn't respond, but that didn't seem to bother Melody at all.

The other girls in the group appeared to be in various stages of terror, curiosity, and acceptance. Heather looked a lot like Irene—dazed and still.

"Okay, everyone, turn to your right!" Deedee commanded in her cheerful, authoritative tone. "Now scrub your friend's back. Give it a good cleaning!"

That brought laughter back to most of the girls. They good-naturedly massaged the person's back in front of them.

"Reverse!" Deedee shouted after a few minutes.

The girls reversed and started their massage again.

*Crack!* The sound split through them. Even Deedee froze in her tracks, looking up the mountainside to see something. Anything. Thunder rolled and rolled—no lightning, just thunder that didn't quit. It started out low, a growl from the throat of the mountain. Gradually it grew into a fierce threat.

Deedee dropped onto a log. Water streamed over her face, her massive curls a waterlogged mess that clumped to her back. China ran and sat next to her. Deedee's eyes were full of fear, her face white. "Landslide," she whispered. "I wish I had binoculars. I can't tell where it is."

China gathered the girls onto the logs. She and the other counselors stood in front of them to form a circle. They held hands. The girls looked at each of the counselors as if they were God and could do something about the weather.

"We're going to pray," China announced.

Misty Meadow seemed to wake up at that. "Let's each pray about something we're thankful for," she said.

China and Deedee looked at her as though she'd lost her mind, but they kept their mouths shut. Any sort of disagreement now would destroy the slim thread holding the girls together.

The rolling landslide grew louder as it approached. China had thought landslides moved fast. Instead, it seemed to move like molasses. Maybe it moved slowly as it gathered rocks, dirt, and trees to push down the mountain. It sounded like a locomotive approaching. The louder it got, the faster it seemed to move.

Deedee whispered in China's ear over Mashiek's frantic prayer of gratitude for a nice mom, dad, sister, and brother—which sounded a lot like a good-bye prayer. "I see it, China," Deedee said. "Up there. It looks like it's following Rattlesnake Creek."

"Huh?" China said. "I didn't know there was another creek."

"It's dry most of the time. It only runs for a little while during snow melt and heavy summer storms like this one. I guess it'll be wider in a few minutes."

"You sound happy about it," China whispered while Mashiek went on and on.

"I am. It means we're safe—sort of."

"What do you mean by that?"

"If it follows Rattlesnake Creek's bed, it will miss us completely."

"What's the sort of?"

"We'll be cut off from the rest of the camp."

China considered this while Misty Meadow encouraged Mashiek to close and let someone else pray.

The ground started to shake. The noise grew so loud that it drowned out a tiny girl's prayer. For a long moment, no one said anything. No one opened her eyes. China prayed and prayed that God would make sure He sent the landslide a different direction. Now she knew it wasn't that the slide moved slowly but that it had started so far up the mountain that made it seem to crawl. By the rumble and crashing that now sounded so close, she knew it moved far too fast and wide and deadly to get out of its way. She looked at her watch and couldn't believe it. Only a few minutes had passed since the initial crack.

"What is that?" Rhonda asked, her voice no more than a whisper.

"Don't be afraid," Deedee said. China thought Deedee sounded like Moses or Michael the archangel. "It's a landslide."

Gasps flowed around the circle.

"But it sounds like it's following the path of Rattlesnake Creek," she added quickly. "If we stay right here, we'll be safe."

Heather glared at Deedee. Heather's black hair was plastered to her face, and mascara blackened her cheeks. "I say we run," she said. "We can escape if we run. How do we know we can trust you?"

Deedee put up her hands—again, like Moses. "Stay put," she responded. "Trust me."

"I've lived here all *my* life, too," Heather said. "I say we run."

Some of the girls nodded, looking at Heather. China noticed that the only girls who looked ready to follow Heather were from her own tepee, plus a few more. She wondered why Deedee didn't contradict Heather's lie.

"You will stay," Deedee said with an authority that everyone listened to—except Heather.

Misty Meadow stepped in front of Heather. "You will obey," Misty commanded.

Heather showed no sign of obeying. Instead, she showed signs of being a terrified filly, ready to bolt. Corrine stepped behind Heather and locked her hands around Heather's wrists. No matter how much Heather struggled, Corrine didn't even look as though she had to try hard to hold her.

"Let go of me!" Heather shrieked above the pounding rain. Her eyes wide with terror, she tried to wham her head backward against Corrine.

"I didn't want to have to do this," Corrine said firmly. She tightened her hold on Heather's wrists and pulled them up the center of her back. Heather dropped to her knees and then fell facedown in the grass.

"I'll kill you for this!" Heather yelled.

The campers stood, staring. They looked smaller

and more fragile in the pelting rain. Their hair had drastically changed their appearance. Their clothes lay plastered to their skin. The little girls shivered, even though the rain wasn't cold.

The landslide rumbled on beyond them. Moments later, the world became eerily silent. The curtain of rain backed off, and Corrine let go of Heather.

In a flash, Heather was on her feet, staring straight into Corrine's eyes. "I promise you," she threatened, "that one day, when your back is turned, you won't know what hit you." Then she took off running down the path.

"Do you think she'll be okay?" Misty Meadow whispered to Deedee.

"I don't know. But we can't chase her down. We've got to take care of these girls first."

Misty nodded. "I'm only a substitute," she confessed quietly. "I don't think they ever figured something this bad would happen. I didn't get the full training like the other leaders."

"It's okay," Deedee said. She turned to the campers. "Girls, I want you all to sit back down on the logs. We'll wait to see if the rain stops. If it does, we should wait an hour or so before returning to camp."

"If it doesn't?" China asked.

"Then we pray and go now."

The girls held hands and didn't say much. Fear kept them silent. At the next bolt of lightning and instant crack of thunder, the girls screamed. A second and third quickly followed. The third crack of thunder was so loud that it sounded as if it broke open the sky. The rain came down in even harder torrents than before.

Deedee gathered the counselors together. "Let's encourage the girls, pray, then head back," she said.

China went to her girls and two of Heather's. She looked each one in the eye and asked how she was. After a hug, she went on to the next one. Melody said she was okay. Mashiek had stopped the dramatics enough to be still. Li kept saying, "It's just like when my family escaped from Vietnam. So dangerous. I'm really scared." Lana held Melody's hand and nodded at everything China said. Irene was fascinated with her waterlogged dress.

"Are you scared, Irene?" China asked.

Irene shrugged and replied, "It doesn't help to be."

"But are you?"

She shrugged again. "I'm here. You're here." She looked up and had to close her eyes against the rain. "God's very noisy, so He's here." She looked at China. "I don't think so."

China didn't mind giving her a hug.

Heather's girls seemed stunned. It was as if their every breath depended on their role model to tell them what to do. Now that she had panicked and disappeared, they had no way to decide anything.

The girls eagerly stood to follow Deedee. China could see trust in all their faces. "Before we go," Deedee announced, "we're going to have Corrine pray."

Corrine smiled as though she stood in the pouring rain every day. She closed her eyes and took the hands of the girls next to her. A chain of hands formed. A row of heads bowed. "God, You're awesome," Corrine began. "Wow. We've been lucky to see Your greatness firsthand today. Kinda goes with what we've been learning."

Small giggles rippled through the ranks.

"You know, some of us down here are kinda nervous. Maybe even scared. I'm glad You're not up there laughing at us. You're down here getting drenched in the rain with us. So we're just askin' You to hold our hands. See to it that we get home safe and sound."

China could feel the hands she held relax just a little.

"And Awesome God," Corrine continued, "Heather's really scared. Can You give her a hug until we can catch up to her?"

There was a long pause.

"Oh, yeah. Amen and all that."

The mood in the group changed to one of giddiness. The girls held hands in a chain and laughed good-naturedly when they slipped and fell in the mud. Misty Meadow had a flash of memory and told them how Indians walk in the rain. After that, they fell less often.

The rain poured on and on, sparking jokes about looking for Noah, animals on the march, and a funny-looking boat. China tilted her head back and drank the water. Her fear had disappeared. She hated being in charge when she was scared. She would have rather curled up in a ball and suffered alone. But when so many kids were looking to her for how they should feel, she had to hide her own fear. Now, however, she showed her real feelings. It felt good to be going back, and good to see the kids losing their fear.

Rounding another bend in the trail, China slowed her pace. She thought she heard Grizzly Creek. Had they made a wrong turn? Did Deedee and Misty get confused with all the rain? It wasn't that big a deal. They would just have to walk farther to get home.

The jokes slowly trailed off as all the girls realized the same thing. Deedee put up her hand. Without another word, the girls stopped.

China tilted her head and listened closely. In the middle of the rushing water, it sounded as if someone was sobbing. She shook her head at the ludicrous thought.

Deedee waved the counselors forward. "Misty, stay here with the girls," she instructed. "The three of us are going to check out the slide."

"That's the slide?" China asked. "I thought it was Grizzly Creek."

Deedee walked ahead without answering. She moved easily over the path, around the turns, and through the trees. As China and Corrine followed, the noise grew louder. China wasn't sure if Grizzly Creek sounded this loud or if the fear of a slide made it sound louder.

Suddenly China's heart stopped. Her blood ran cold. Tingling pricked the back of her neck. She'd read about all the sensations before, but she'd never felt them. Instead of a nice trail meandering through the many trees, there was an ugly gash. Rocks and boulders the size of garbage cans and small cars lay about as if they had always been there. Uprooted trees stuck out at awkward angles, broken and shredded like toothpicks. Muddy water poured down the mountain, splashing over the boulders and between the trees. China felt as if she were witness to a brutal murder.

As she drew near to Deedee, the two of them linked pinkies.

Even Corrine looked shaken by the power of the slide. "Can it get worse?" she asked.

"I don't know," Deedee breathed.

China cocked her head. She closed her eyes to block out the ugly sight so that she could listen. Someone was definitely sobbing.

## CHAPTER NINE

**D**EEDEE STOOD, hands on hips, staring at the slide.

"Deeds, someone's crying," China said. "It's Heather, I'll bet."

"Shhh." Deedee put her hand up and kept staring. She turned to Corrine and said, "You're strong. Are you brave?"

Corrine smiled.

"I'm not," China quipped.

"Too bad," Deedee said. "But one brave person is all we need." She turned away and stared again at the slide. "I think we can do it." She began to pace up and down the edge. "Look. Over there. It's wider. We'll put one person on each rock."

"Won't they be slippery?" China asked.

"They haven't been underwater long. They should be okay. We'll hand the kids over and get them across. These girls are pretty small."

"Except Irene," China reminded her.

Deedee frowned. "That is a problem."

"You aren't very strong," China said, putting her hand on Deedee's arm.

"I'll be the ground person here," Deedee said. "I'll help the kids onto the rock where you can grab them." She stood on a rock that had been kicked aside by the slide. "Misty'll be on that rock there. We'll put Corrine on the final leg. She'll have to do the most work." Deedee looked at Corrine. "Can you do that? Swing them from Misty to you to the safe side?"

"No problem."

"Now, if we can get Heather to take charge on the other side . . ."

China turned toward the sounds of crying, then looked back at Deedee. "You've got to be kidding," China said.

Deedee shrugged. "Why not? Giving her some responsibility might make her sane again."

"She wasn't sane in the first place."

"Go get her," Deedee said.

"Why not send Corrine?"

"She's going to kill Corrine, remember?"

"Well, I'm not sure she won't kill me, too."

"I'll make sure you get a nice tombstone."

"Thanks, Deeds. You're a pal."

China wished the rain would stop. It poured down her face, in her ears, and made it difficult to see. Her clothes weighed a ton. "Heather?" she called, pushing aside tree branches. She waited, listening for sobs. But they had stopped. "Heather."

"Go away," Heather said.

China turned a little to the right, trying to see where Heather was. "Heather," she called, "we need you." China felt like gagging on her words. At least they weren't a lie.

"Go away," Heather insisted. "We're all going to die. Every last one of us. I'm going to kill my father."

"If you die, you can't kill him. So you'd better come with us so you can kill him properly." China wanted to keep Heather mad, keep her talking. She knew she'd find her at any moment if she kept talking.

"You think you're so funny, China Tate. Well, I hate you. You can die, too, for all I care."

China walked around a huge boulder and looked down at a muddy Heather. She had wrapped her arms tightly around herself and curled up against the smooth granite. China let herself feel sorry for Heather. She knew the feeling wouldn't last long anyway; Heather would see to that.

China squatted in front of Heather. "Look," China said, "we really do need you. Deedee has it all figured out. There's a wide spot in the slide where there's good, solid rocks to stand on. We'll pass the kids across the water."

"So what do you need me for?"

"To be the one who gets the kids on the other side."

Heather thought about it. "So you guys are going to let me be the guinea pig. If I don't fall in and get washed away, it's safe for you guys."

China rolled her eyes and began to get impatient. "Not if you don't want," she said. "We'll all be at our posts, and we'll help you across."

Heather looked at her manicured nails and flicked caked mud out from under them. "Well, all right," she finally said.

China thought she'd fall over dead in shock.

By the time they got to the slide, Deedee had returned with all the little Indians. Deedee winked at China. Corrine had to go first, pausing at each step. She looked up the slide ravine and shivered. She looked downstream. Then she looked ahead at her next step. When she got to her final boulder, she gave them a thumbs-up.

Misty followed, not looking at anything but her feet. China could see her shake. Misty pressed her lips tight but didn't show any other emotion. She only nodded when she reached her perch. She still didn't look anywhere but at her feet.

China didn't have far to go. But still her heart beat so fast she could hardly see. The water seemed colder than the rain. It stung her bare legs. The first boulder remained firm under her feet. She stretched her long legs over to the second and stood still. Her boulder was wide and flat. Water flowed in a thin sheet over the top, but it stood firm. There was room to move on it. There was room for a mistake.

She put out her hand and looked at Heather. Deedee stood behind her so she couldn't bolt very easily.

She whispered something into Heather's ear.

"As if *that's* going to help," Heather snapped.

Deedee moved forward, urging Heather forward at the same time. Heather looked at her three anchors. China looked weak but was in fact quite strong. Misty still wouldn't glance up from her feet. Corrine was built like a rock herself.

Heather reached out and grasped China's hand. Heather's hand was cold and clammy, and her nails dug into China. Heather didn't look at her. She moved her feet in tiny baby shuffles. When she got to the other side of China, she reached her other hand out to Misty without letting go of China. She stood there a moment, one hand holding on to each girl, her arms stretched as far as they would go.

"Let go," China said.

"I can't," Heather insisted.

"Let go, Heather," Deedee demanded.

"It's okay. I have you," Misty encouraged.

Heather's grip tightened on China's hand.

"Let go," China said louder.

Heather didn't. She stood spread-eagled.

China peeled Heather's fingers back and pushed her own hand down at the same time. Her arm slid free. Heather screamed, threw her arm in the air, and slipped. Everyone gasped as Misty held on tight and pulled Heather onto the rock beside her.

Heather turned to glare at China. "You tried to kill me!" she accused.

China shook her head. "You can't move on if you don't let go."

Anger swelled in Heather. She stood taller and took one giant step toward Corrine, using Corrine's arm for leverage. Then she took one flying leap to the trail beyond. She slipped again, falling against a rock. Blood trickled down her leg. She stared at it, then looked up at the rescuers. "You guys can save yourselves!" she shouted. And then she flounced off.

"Heather!" Deedee shouted over the water. "Come back!"

Heather turned and gave a quick look. She stuck her chin in the air and fled.

"What now?" China asked.

"We do it without her," Deedee answered.

Mashiek volunteered to go first. Deedee steadied her on shore while Mashiek leaned out to China. China grabbed her wrist and pulled her toward the rock. Mashiek swung through the open air and landed solidly next to China.

"Good girl," China whispered to her.

Mashiek grinned from ear to ear. China got another firm grip on her wrist and swung her out to Misty. Misty grabbed her and steadied her while Mashiek put her foot on a rock. Corrine, without any trouble whatsoever, grabbed Mashiek. In one long move, she picked her up and set her down on shore.

The rescuers started a rhythm. It became easier with each girl. Their confidence rose, and the remaining girls no longer seemed afraid.

Irene lingered in the back until all the other girls were across. Deedee turned to her. "You can't lift me," Irene said plainly. "I can make it by myself." She wobbled over to the edge of the slide and put her chubby hands on her hips. "We can't both fit," she told China.

China looked at her perch and nodded. But now she was afraid. What if Irene fell? How would they tell her parents? Misty had already moved to the far side. Corrine remained at her post. There was nothing left for China to do but move across the slide. At each boulder, she waited for Irene to move to the next perch. Deedee followed right behind.

Irene did everything in a way that looked as though she had no sense of balance. She paused before each step as though she had to think through every move first. But as she did everything else in life, she paid attention to detail and made steady progress.

China was grateful for Corrine's strong grip to help her across the final gap. Corrine also helped Irene, then Deedee. When Corrine jumped to the ground, everyone cheered.

The rain still pounded them. The ground still mushed and gushed under them. But the fear was gone. A deep peace and joy spread through the group and stayed with them. Misty took her place at the front of the line and led the girls home. They sang every song they knew at the top of their lungs.

After some time, China noticed movement in the

trees behind them. Farther back down the line, Deedee flashed a wide grin. China cocked her head,
silently asking, "What?"

Deedee mouthed, "Heather."

China cocked her head to the other side. "Heather?"

Deedee nodded and tried not to laugh. China
wagged her head and rolled her eyes.

By the time the girls had reached the Tribal Village,
the rain had calmed to a regular, steady beat. Eagerly
they disappeared into their tepees, stripped down,
dried off, and changed into dry clothes.

By this time, Mashiek had regained all her dramatics. "We could have *died* out there!" she said. "Oh,
my goodness! Did you see all that water?"

The girls were talkative and full of laughter—
except, of course, for Irene. She carefully peeled off
her wet things and replaced them with dry clothes—
without taking off her wet underclothes first. Within
minutes, she had a round, wet spot on the back of her
dress and three round, wet spots on the front.

"Can we come in?" Rhonda asked plaintively at the
door. She looked like a drowned critter, not a child.
"Our tepee is all wet."

"What?" China said. She had been so busy getting
dry that she hadn't even noticed if water had come
into their tepee. The center had a small puddle where
a few drops had come in. She couldn't understand
how Water tepee had lived up to its name.

She motioned to Rhonda and said, "Sure, honey,

come on in." *Oh, my*, she thought. *I'm turning into Magda*. She got the girls situated and then ran over to Water tepee and looked in.

Before they had left for the hike, no one had bothered to roll the tepee sides down, guaranteeing a watery mess from the rain. But the carpet seemed to be the worst culprit. It acted like a sponge, soaking in and holding gallons of water. The tepee was uninhabitable.

"Do you *mind?*" Heather asked, holding a towel up in front of her.

China whirled around and returned to her tepee. "Come on, girls," she told her kids. "Our sisters need our help again." China's girls followed her to Water tepee, where they gathered up all the belongings they found there. Heather guarded her own things, so they left those. Anything wet they put in Earth tepee to dry. Everything else they put in Sky tepee—Heather's girls' new home. Some of the girls got wet enough to change clothes again, but no one seemed upset or put off by it.

Heather's girls seemed sodden in spirit as well as body. China felt sorry for them. Their leader had disappointed them again and again.

Both groups ate lunch in Rock tepee. Heather had disappeared once again. No one asked where she might be.

After lunch, Sky tepee swept the floor of Rock tepee, eager to repay the girls for their kindness. With cleanup over, the girls had a whole afternoon of free time available to them. China didn't know what to do with 10 little Indians on a rainy day without games to play. She consulted her counselor's guide and discovered they could go to the Long House for crafts.

As they marched up the hill, they saw that three white vans had invaded the Tribal Village. All three had huge contraptions on them that looked like satellite dishes or space gadgets. The letters ABC were painted on the side of one van. CBS and NBC were painted on the others. The girls started talking in a flurry of excitement. News crews? What were they doing at the Tribal Village?

Without thinking, China sped up, her little charges right on her heels.

## CHAPTER TEN

**K**IDS JAMMED INSIDE LONG HOUSE. China could barely squeeze past them. Just as her group managed to get in, Deedee showed up with her kids. Corrine followed with hers.

"What's going on?" Deedee asked.

"I don't know," China said.

"Some girl saved a bunch of kids," a boy near them said. "So the TV guys came to talk to her. It's real cool."

"Why did they come here?"

The kid shrugged. "I guess because they were Tribal Village kids."

A shot of electricity zoomed through China. She strained to see around the huge guy counselors blocking her view. Kids swarmed around her like a zillion little bees.

"Excuse me," Deedee said loudly. "We shrimps can't see back here."

"Yeah," all the little guys chimed in. "Down in front," they started to chant. "Down in front."

Crouching down, the tall guys immediately became short guys. Now China could see all the way to the front. She turned and stared at Deedee. Together they said, *"Heather?"*

Corrine crossed her arms. "What's she up to now?" she asked.

The bright television lights went on. Heather looked gorgeous—not a hair out of place. In the back of Long House, the girls couldn't hear what the news reporters were saying into their little microphones. Heather smiled, turning from side to side, slowly licking her lips. She looked like a model.

"What is she doing?" Corrine asked, having never really seen Heather in action.

"Shhh," China and Deedee replied together.

Heather nodded at something one of the newscasters said. She pointed down at her leg. China stood on tiptoe. Heather had cleaned her whole body except for that one part of her leg. Dried blood caked there, making the wound look far more gruesome than it was.

"Maybe we should do a DNA test to see if it's really her blood," Corrine said, her arms crossed even tighter.

"Shhh," came the unified response.

"It was terrifying," Heather said, her arms waving around dramatically yet still controlled. "Water cascading like a giant wall down the mountainside. Huge raindrops pelting us in torrents. The girls screamed in terror. But I calmed them with my love and gentle voice."

China felt a kind of bizarre fog descend on her brain. *This can't be happening,* she thought.

"The other counselors huddled in fear . . ."

*"What?"* shrieked Corrine. "Let me at her! I'm going to tear her limb from limb." But she stood there as frozen with unbelief as China and Deedee.

"I single-handedly carried those children over the precipice, one by one."

"Are those children here? Can we speak to them?"

"Oh no. Most are too traumatized by what happened. I did bring one."

A small, plain-looking girl stood next to Heather. China recognized her as a kid from another tribe who had been following Heather around the council fire. Her eyes were always wide with wonder. Before today, Heather had always told her to get lost and then ignored her. Now it looked as though the child's adoration was paying off for Heather.

In a rehearsed monotone, the little girl recited her speech. "It was absolutely amazing," she said. "This counselor risked her life for all of us girls." She looked up at Heather, who nodded her encouragement. "She hurt her leg risking her life."

"Were you scared?"

The girl nodded.

"What did the landslide look like?"

The girl looked frantically at Heather.

"It had huge boulders, broken trees, and lots of water," Heather answered for her.

"The water was cold," the little girl offered.

Corrine started forward through the crowd. China and Deedee followed. "It's a lie!" Corrine shouted.

Heather gave a full-blown Heather-smile. There was nothing on earth quite like it, full of confidence, authority, and pity, all rolled into one. "Oh, here come the other counselors," she said. "I'm sure they feel badly about how they acted. I would like to say publicly that there is no shame in fear. But for a lucky few, fear is not an option." She put on that smile again, gazing condescendingly at the counselors.

Corrine's red face and clenched fists gave China the impression she was about to explode. China figured touching her was not a wise option at the moment. So she leaned as close as she could and whispered, "Don't fight it right now. She's got all the tools to win."

"Except the truth," Corrine hissed.

"Trust me. She's gifted. She can take any truth and bury it so no one finds it."

Corrine spun around and marched out. Her tepee of girls trailed along after her. China and Deedee retreated to the back of the room, wanting to hear the rest. But there was no more.

"Why don't you fight her?" Mashiek asked. "Go beat her up. *You* should be on TV, not her."

China felt suddenly calm. She knelt down and looked Mashiek in the eyes. "The truth will eventually come out," she said. "Besides, it's not that important.

Deedee and I don't want to be on TV anyway. We did what was best, and nothing else matters."

A warm peace began to fill China. All the things she'd been through in the past weeks came back to her. The stupid things. The good things. She'd actually learned something. She smiled and linked pinkies with Deedee.

Heather's girls looked confused and glum. "We coulda lied for her, too," one pouted. "Then we coulda been on TV."

"I ain't lying for nobody," Rhonda said. "If God's big enough to flick the sun like a marble, I ain't stupid enough to go messing with Him by lying."

"Let's find the crafts," Deedee suggested.

The girls created the afternoon away. Some painted leather for key chains, belts, and wall hangings. Some beaded necklaces and hairbands. China felt too klutzy with all that, so she chose user-friendly plastic to make odd shapes into jewelry her mother and grandmother might wear out of kindness. While the plastic softened and shrunk in a hot water bath, her mind refused to relax. It tossed questions at her that were interesting but unanswerable: *Why would Heather lie about an event where so many others saw a different truth? Why does Heather hate me so much? Why is Heather so much like . . . like . . . Heather?*

China's thoughts were interrupted by eager girls who needed help on their projects, as well as by proud girls who wanted to show theirs off. The giggling and constant chatter were enough to keep China's brain from focusing on any one thing for too long. Only once was she able to get close enough to Deedee to whisper a furtive, "Why would she do that?"

"I have no clue," Deedee replied.

The campers ate dinner in their tepees, the rain beating steadily on the canvas walls. That night, the council fire was held in Long House. The Indians sat cross-legged while Chief Black Bear incorporated the wild rain and landslide into his talk about the great God who cares about small details and about each camper individually.

While Chief Black Bear spoke, China looked up as a door opened. Mr. Kiersey's face peered in, scoping the room, looking for something. When he saw China, he winked. He pointed to Deedee. China poked Deedee, who saw her father and left. About 10 minutes later, she returned. "Dad wanted to know what happened this afternoon," she whispered in China's ear. "They have to report all incidents to the county and also have records of it on file. Someone called and told him about Heather being on TV."

"Does he believe you?"

Deedee made a face. "Of course he believes me," she said. "After the fiasco at the beginning of the summer, he will check things out more thoroughly before he believes Heather again."

China turned her thoughts back to the chief. It felt

good to be believed. It felt good to know that probably the only person in authority who really mattered
knew the truth.

Back in the tepee later, the girls were more eager
than before to listen to China read the Bible. Each one
thanked God for a safe return to their temporary
home.

China didn't tell the girls what she'd learned after
the council fire. God really had been with them. If
they had tried to go back to the Tribal Village earlier
and beat the rain, they could have been caught in the
slide. A tree along the trail had been split by lightning.
What if they'd been there then?

The other lead counselors had checked the weather
that morning right before leaving—as they were
supposed to do—and had avoided the storm in Long
House. No one thought much about the other tribes
being gone. If Singing Bird had decided to take them
out, then all was well. Singing Bird knew more about
the mountains than anyone. But they didn't know she
had taken ill and that Misty, the least-experienced
leader, had taken the group up the mountain.

China settled on her cot, snuggling down into her
sleeping bag. The whispers and stifled giggles of the
girls were a pleasant period at the end of an exhausting day.

Snores soon erupted from Irene's bed, effectively
smothering the peaceful twilight of sleep.

"Someone shut her up," Mashiek said.

"She sounds like a pig going for food," Lana said, then dissolved into a giggle. "Snort, snort, snorkel, snort."

The other girls muffled bursts of laughter behind their hands and under their pillows.

"Girls," China reprimanded. "Be nice."

"Why should we?" Li asked. "She's not nice to us."

"She's so *stupid*," Mashiek added. "She picks her nose—"

"And picks her toes," Lana rhymed.

"And wears bras over boobs she doesn't even have," Melody said, sounding a little ashamed she said it. "At least she doesn't stink anymore after today's forced shower."

All the girls giggled again.

"She doesn't even have a brain," Li said. "I think she must be a retard or something."

"Li!" China hissed. "I can't believe you said that. All you girls. I'm ashamed of you." *Oh, gross,* she thought. *I'm sounding like my mother again. But I don't know what to do unless I do it like my mother would.* Then she told the girls, "We should love people no matter what. Jesus told us to love our enemies, love the people who are unlovely, different, or slow."

"You don't," Lana said pointedly.

China bolted upright on her cot. "What do you mean?" she asked.

"You don't love Irene."

"Yeah," Mashiek joined in. "You don't like her, either."

China swallowed. They were right. Irene, as much as China figured she was supposed to make a difference in the girl's life, was a total pain. She wasn't responding to any of China's efforts to include her, guide her, or direct her. She appeared to have no redeeming qualities. But how did the girls know she thought that?

"You treat her just like we do," Lana said firmly.

"I don't make fun of her," China protested.

"Except for that, you ignore her just as much as we do."

"You treat her like a pet dog," Li said. "You feed her, tell her where to go, and just make sure no one is cruel to her."

China was glad the dark hid her blushing face. Another mother-thought popped into her head. "Why don't we each think of one nice thing about Irene," she suggested. "Anyone?"

Long silence.

"You go first," Lana said.

China hadn't counted on that. "Okay," she said, hoping that would bring something to mind. She thought over the past couple of days, trying to find anything at all to focus on. Nothing good came to mind.

"We'll be asleep before you think of anything," Mashiek said.

Then one thought came to China's mind. "She's God's child," China said.

A pillow smacked her in the head. "That's cheating!" Li said in her high-pitched voice.

"What a lame answer!" Mashiek said.

The snoring stopped. Everyone instantly became quiet. Irene shifted in her bed, then resumed snoring.

Not wanting to sound defensive but knowing in the end it was true, China defended her answer. "God cares about each person," she said. "He made each person in the shape and—"

"But Irene stretched her shape with too much eating," Li interrupted.

Giggles.

"But He made the inside of her somehow in His image," China resumed. "Everyone was made with something of God as a part of them." Even as the words popped out of China's mouth, she wondered what part of God could possibly be in Irene.

"Irene—like God?" Lana said, bursting into a laugh.

"Is God fat?" Li asked.

"And stupid?" Mashiek said.

"Maybe we'll just have to look for something of God in Irene during the rest of the week," China said. "The first person who thinks of a good one gets a candy bar."

They liked that.

"Can you think of something else?" China encouraged. "Something that's likable about Irene?"

Another long silence.

"She doesn't swear," Melody said. "I've heard a lot of kids from other tribes swearing. I'm glad she doesn't."

"Okay!" China said a little too enthusiastically. "She doesn't swear. Anything else?"

The girls thought and thought, and without another word, every one of them fell asleep. And Irene snored.

## CHAPTER ELEVEN

THE RAIN STOPPED SOMETIME in the night. The girls woke to three drumbeats and a cloudless sky. China donated her towel to wipe down the picnic tables so they could eat outside. Everyone took turns staring at Irene, as if a good, hard look might yield the answer to China's question of the night before. Even China caught herself investigating every inch of Irene. She found herself thinking terrible thoughts, such as *If this is what God looks like, He'd better be extra nice so people will like Him.*

Heather's girls looked sodden in spirit. They tried to perk up as they listened to Heather's intricate instructions on how to behave as young, pretty girls out to catch a guy. As the day progressed, most of the girls warmed up to the idea once again. Rhonda was the lone holdout, always standing at a distance, arms crossed, eyes narrowed. Her only look of interest and longing was cast in the direction of Rock tepee.

Singing Bird was back. The girls were eager to tell

the story of what happened the day before, and Singing Bird was eager to hear it. Heather glowered at the girls who said the counselors helped carry them across the raging waters. But no one told Singing Bird about Heather's lie. They gave Heather sideways glances and didn't mention that she had run away.

China hoped the truth would eventually come out. Heather's abandonment of her girls proved she was not fit to be a counselor.

Singing Bird took them on a short morning hike in the opposite direction from the previous day's hike. Her soothing voice and compelling knowledge of nature and Indian lore kept the girls spellbound. They especially liked the part about edible plants, even though they made gagging sounds and said "Eeewww" with every new lunch possibility.

"God cares about our needs," Singing Bird said. "He provides for them."

"With plants?" Mashiek said. "Yuck."

"He doesn't always provide in ways that are like a gourmet meal," Singing Bird told her gently. "But He always provides."

China nodded. Her missionary-barrel clothes were evidence of that. They were never in style, but at least they covered her body.

"I ate bugs before," Irene said in her monotone. "They crunch a lot, but they don't really fill you up."

Singing Bird agreed, then went on to tell them about which bugs were edible. That grossed out the girls even more than before.

When they returned to the tribe, China wasn't too sure lunch sounded appetizing. All the girls seemed to think there might be hidden plants or bugs in the hamburgers.

"These are really squashed, fried bugs!" Rhonda said, waving a potato chip. She chomped down on it. "Yum!"

"Gross!" screamed Lana.

"And this," another of Heather's girls cried, holding up her hamburger, "is plants and bugs mixed together. We spread bug juice on them to make them taste better!"

"You are so sick!" Li said, chucking a potato chip at her.

A piece of hamburger sailed back, and Li ducked. Before China could even take in a breath, tiny bits of food were flying all over.

"This isn't very ladylike, girls," Heather said to her charges.

No one listened.

"No food fights!" China shouted.

The rain of food ceased. Julie, however, dipped her fingers into her cup and flicked punch drops on Laura. Laura dipped her fingers but missed Julie and hit Jenny. Quickly, punch drops were raining everywhere, mingled with excited laughter.

Julie refilled her cup at the jug.

"This is ridiculous," Heather said. "I can't believe

you little heathens are in my tepee." She gathered her own plate and punch cup and lifted her leg to step over the picnic bench. A French fry zoomed by her head just then, and she flinched to get out of the way. Distracted, she didn't quite clear the bench with her foot. One shining moment she was standing, the next she was in the dirt with one leg propped on the bench. Her cup of punch and its contents had attacked her chest, right below the neckline.

Ten-year-old girls have a tendency to laugh loud and often. And this bunch didn't hesitate to act their age. China tried to stuff her laugh, but it kept oozing out.

Heather untangled her leg and stood quickly. China could see she was ready to explode. "Who did this?" Heather demanded, looking for someone other than herself to blame.

In the middle of Heather's chest, a red splotch started to grow from the inside out. A separate splotch appeared somewhere high on her stomach.

"Look!" Mashiek cried through her guffaws. "The punch has started a new riverbed—right down the middle of Heather!"

At that, Heather dropped her plate and cup into the dirt and marched toward her tepee. Moments later, she reappeared, waltzing up to the washing trough wrapped in a towel. She put a washcloth to good use and then disappeared into the tepee again. Within five minutes, she was back, looking as if nothing had happened. She wore a new outfit—white shorts with a pink and white crop top. The top strands of her hair were pulled back into a bright barrette.

"Come on, girls," she said. "Let's go to the pool."

Like a swarm of small bees, the girls cleaned up from lunch, gathered their things, and were gone. The afternoon passed in a blur of creek walking, sunbathing, and gorging on junk food. After dinner, the girls sang their hearts out at the council fire. By bedtime, no one had come up with any positive things to say about Irene.

Singing Bird's voice ended the day with her song that lulled them all to silence. The story-song made them want to be still and listen. Being still made them hear the call of sleep, and each one drifted off.

China's eyelids popped open at the sound of the voice—the only voice that could sound like that at 7:00 in the morning.

"All right, who did it?"

China could hear tones of protest coming from Sky tepee.

"I want to know *who* did it!"

China closed her eyes and counted, waiting for Heather to burst into her tepee. *One-one thousand, two-one thousand, three—*

"Which one of you creeps did it?" Heather demanded at their tepee door.

*Three seconds,* China thought. *She's getting a little slow.*

Heather marched right in and began rifling through the girls' things, throwing clothes this way and that. "I know you think these little jokes are clever," she said, "but they're *stupid.* So you can just give it back, right now."

China rolled onto her side. Heather's dramatics were really beginning to irritate her. "Heather, stop it," she said. It must have been the unexpected calm tone of authority that stopped Heather in her tracks. "What are you looking for?"

"Your little brats know *exactly* what I'm looking for." She glared at each one in turn. Irene was pulling socks out of her suitcase one at a time, smelling them before she laid them down again. "You!" Heather said, pointing a long, skinny finger at Irene. "You look at me!"

Irene, oblivious to the rest of the world, continued to smell her socks.

"You don't fool me," Heather said.

China sighed and got out of bed. She padded over to Heather and told her, "She didn't take anything."

"How can you be so sure?"

"She doesn't have a thief bone in her body. I think she's incapable of taking something that isn't hers."

"That's it!" one of China's girls shouted. "That's the God part!"

China grinned. "You're right," she said. "God never takes something that doesn't belong to Him. Of course, all things belong to Him."

"I suppose you're going to tell me God wants to wear my bra!" Heather shouted.

The girls instantly quieted. They stared at Heather with expressions that said, "Did she say what I thought she said?"

Heather blushed in the silence.

China looked Heather in the eyes and asked, "What do you think we took?"

"Not think. Know."

China just continued to look at Heather.

"My bra."

China glanced around at her girls. By their faces, she knew they didn't know anything about it. "We have no reason to take your bra," China said. Then she couldn't resist. "There's not a one of us who could fill it like you."

The girls sputtered. Heather's eyes narrowed.

China put her hands on her hips and tilted her head. "Don't you recognize a compliment when you hear one?" she said.

Heather looked confused.

China took the clothes out of Heather's hand and gently moved her toward the door. "Maybe you just can't find it in your stuff. Maybe it's in your sleeping bag."

"I laid it on the tepee yesterday after lunch to dry."

China felt as if she were dealing with another 10-year-old and that she had just been promoted to mother. "Come on. Let's go look."

The whole group padded out in socks and bare feet to Sky tepee. China looked on the ground where the tepee met it. She stuck her hand in under the canvas and felt around.

"What's that?" called a male voice just then.

The girls scattered, shrieking, as a whole line of boys from another tribe stopped and looked up into a tree beyond them.

"Wow!" one smart aleck called. "I wondered where those things came from. Looks like they grow on trees."

"It's a big one!" called another mouth.

"Ooohhh, Ooohhh, Ooohhh," they all started.

"What are they talking about?" Heather demanded.

"Over here!" Li called. She pointed into a tree. There hung Heather's now-pink bra like a Christmas ornament.

Heather gasped, turned to look at the boys, then back at the bra, then back at the boys again, who still cackled and cat-called and woofed. Her hands popped to her hips. "What're you staring at?" she challenged.

"A new type of tree," they called. Heather's venom obviously didn't faze them. "Best one we've seen in a long time."

Frustrated, Heather turned to vent on China. "See? Your girl knew right where it was." She turned to Li. "Since you put it there, you have to go get it for me."

"I didn't put it anywhere," Li protested before she marched off. Over her shoulder she called, "Didn't anyone ever teach you manners? You could at least say thank you."

"Spoiled brat," Heather muttered under her breath.

China shook her head, amazed. "The boys pointed it out," she said.

"But your girl was there in an instant."

"Give it up, Heather."

Melody climbed the tree and brought it down. She handed it to Heather as if it were a piece of dirty underwear. Well, it *was* stained and dirty.

"Did you wash it before you hung it out?" China asked.

"That's none of your business."

"I just thought that since the 'coons were lured here once by candy, maybe they came back to try again. What they found smelled like sugar, but it didn't taste quite right."

"Oh, and you're such an expert on wild animal behavior," Heather said sarcastically.

China felt her heart grow cold at the memory of the bears. "I've learned a lot since I've been here," she managed to say.

## CHAPTER TWELVE

CHINA FELT ALL HER ENERGY, renewed by a
night of sleep, drain away. As she went to her tepee to
get dressed, she became painfully aware that this job
placed too many demands on her.

Wanting to make a difference in someone else's life
was hard work. And China felt frustrated that her
deepest desire for the week got put on hold just so
she could keep up with the demands that met her at
every moment: defusing petty fights, fielding questions, trying to answer questions that have no answer,
admitting defeat, picking up, cleaning up, going
from meeting to hiking to playing games, laughing at
bad jokes, feigning interest in who said what to whom
as the results were relayed in excited gunshot volleys
of words between girls, and keeping one corner of
her eye on Heather in order to be prepared for anything. And still, lurking in the back of her mind, waiting impatiently, was the desperate desire to make a
difference in someone's life. But how do you fulfill

a desperate desire when the tyranny of the urgent crowds it out?

The day proceeded at an exhausting pace. China wanted nothing more than to stretch out on her cot and go to sleep. But the day hadn't ended yet, and the demands hadn't ceased—they only changed direction.

China didn't like the fact that she was on her own in this. She much preferred sharing things with Deedee. But the Tribal Village kept them apart for most of the day. When they spent any moments together, they shared them with chatty, giggling, opinionated, demanding girls. On the other side of camp, Magda bustled about her kitchen with words of wisdom that sat just beneath the surface, ready to pop out when China needed them most. But there was no phone in Rock tepee. There was no phone in all the Tribal Village.

Worse, China's girls wanted to go to the lake, while Deedee's girls wanted to make more crafts. "No stolen moments of conversation," Deedee said with an exaggerated pout.

"I suppose we'll live," China replied.

Deedee smiled. "Rendezvous," she said like a spy. "Under the huge oak at the turn near Sioux for our free time during powwow. We'll have 90 minutes, just you and me."

China looked around to see if anyone had heard. She couldn't think what spies were supposed to say in response to a secret rendezvous plan, so she just stuck up her thumb.

When her happy little group reached the lake, one by one their laughter turned to silence. Heather and her girls lay in two perfect rows. It seemed they were there for another lesson—*how to lie on the beach and attract all the guys.* One by one, then two by two, high school guys approached Heather, trying their best to win her attention.

"This is disgusting," Mashiek said. "I'm going to jump on the Blob."

Everyone except Irene trotted through the hot sand to wade in the waters of Little Bear Lake. They made China agree to go off the Blob first to make sure they wouldn't all die. China rolled her eyes at their fears. Without hesitation, she stood at the edge of the platform and jumped onto the huge, air-filled pillow. She scrambled to the edge and was propelled into the air when the next girl landed on the Blob. She splashed into the water, then swam toward the platform for another round. Within minutes, all the girls had taken a turn and were lining up for more. After three times blobbing, China returned to the beach.

"It's not a good thing," Heather was saying to her girls. "Do you see how unladylike every one of those girls looks? All sprawled every which way? Don't go. It will ruin your reputation."

"I am not a potato," Rhonda said. "Baking is not for me. I'm going to have fun." She marched off with all but two girls following her.

The two girls who remained behind looked torn

between staying and going. Heather's praise kept them on their towels.

China sat on her towel and searched for Irene. She found her sitting at the edge of the water. She repeatedly poked a finger into the sand and watched the girls blob.

China lay on her stomach, propping herself up on her elbows. The hot sun made her squint. Mashiek seemed to be organizing Heather's girls, lining everyone up so the opposing tepees would blob each other.

China let her thoughts wander. She watched the scene before her at the same time she thought of a zillion things popping in and out of her head. What finally caught her attention was a pudgy girl mounting the steps to the Blob tower. *Irene?* she thought. *I didn't know Irene could swim.*

China sat up to get a closer look. A little kid waited at the top, then scurried down the ladder. Without waiting for instructions from the lifeguard, Irene lumbered forward. Whistles blew. A bullhorn blared "Stop!" But China knew Irene heard nothing. She went to the edge of the platform and was off before anyone could grab her.

When she landed on one end of the Blob, a much smaller body flew off the other. The smaller girl's scream and takeoff were one indication that she wasn't ready. Her belly flop landing confirmed it. The lifeguard was off her tower and in the water before the girl even landed, and she helped the girl to shore.

China shivered. *Laura. Heather's tiniest camper.*

China ran across the sand and crouched down in front of Laura. "Are you okay?" she asked, looking directly into Laura's eyes.

Laura nodded. She sat on the shore, shaking inside her towel. Her teeth chattered. All of her friends gathered around her. "Are you okay, Laura?" they asked.

Beyond the little girl, China could see the lifeguard guiding Irene safely back to the sandy beach. China rubbed Laura's back and said, "I don't think Irene meant to hurt you. She gets so focused on one thing that she doesn't see or hear what's going on around her."

Laura nodded again. "I know that," she said in a soft whisper. Then she smiled weakly. "It would've been fun if I'd been a little more prepared."

A looming shadow covered them. "This is not funny, China Tate," Heather scolded. "I've had it with your antics and your vicious responses. How dare you try to hurt one of *my* girls?"

China looked up at Heather. She wanted to ask "How did I hurt one of your girls?" but she knew the question wouldn't compute with Heather, who had things all twisted in her mind. Instead, she said, "I wouldn't hurt one of your girls."

Laura shook her head and said, "She didn't do anything, Heather."

"Shut up," Heather snapped. "You don't know anything."

Tears came to Laura's eyes, while Heather continued

to attack China. "How *dare* you try to get back at me by taking it out on an innocent child!"

"I'm not that vindictive, Heather," China protested, her own sweet attitude taking a quick hike.

"You try to be a sweet-looking Christian girl," Heather spewed. "But in reality, you're no different from the scum that inhabit the rest of the world. I can't believe Mr. Kiersey was so fooled by you."

Ignoring Heather, China looked at Laura and said, "Again, Laura, I'm sorry it happened. I'm glad you're okay." Then she and the girls from Rock tepee walked silently to their patchwork of towels. Irene sat there, picking her wet suit off her body and letting it slap against her skin. It must have been reassuring somehow, for she did it over and over. Then she got up and walked to the water's edge, where she poured wet sand on her legs over and over.

"Why does Heather hate you?" Mashiek asked.

China sighed and looked at the ground. She found a tiny stick and began to draw in the hot sand. She paused, thinking back to her first week at Camp Crazy Bear. She shrugged. "We met here at the beginning of summer," she finally said. "I was different. I wore funny clothes."

"You still do," Mashiek commented.

China playfully whacked her head. "I also wasn't pretty."

"You are, too," Li said.

"Not like Heather," China said.

Li sobered. "No, not like Heather."

*Well, I guess I'm glad she's honest,* China thought.

"Anyway, I didn't fit into her little group." China hesitated. She could leave it at that, or she could tell the whole truth. Anything short would be deceiving. She went on. "I got mad at her, and I wasn't very nice. When I finally decided I wasn't acting the way God wanted me to act, it was too late. Things got pretty bad after that."

The girls sat around her, no one saying a word.

"I was mean to someone once," Mashiek said after a minute, as if to make it easier for China.

The rest of the girls snickered. "Once?" Li asked. "Only once?"

Mashiek lifted her chin, looking indignant. "Never mind. I was going to tell the story, but never mind."

No amount of coaxing brought Mashiek's chin down even one tiny bit or got her to tell the story. China glanced at the watch Deedee had loaned her. "Time to go, girls."

The girls moaned their protests. China took Irene's towel to her and told her it was time to go. *Another good thing about Irene,* she thought. *She obeys.*

They paused at the creek during the long, hot walk back. They soaked their dry towels in the cold water and wrapped them around their shoulders. Irene soaked hers, too. But no matter how much China coaxed her, she still dragged a third of it through the dirt all the way back to the tepee.

Their tepee was soon covered with towels drying in the sun. China kissed all her girls on the tops of their heads. She hesitated at Irene, then squeezed her eyes shut, forcing herself to do it.

Deedee was already at the oak tree when China got there, waiting for her. "I'm whupped," China told her. "Can we just go sit somewhere?"

Deedee frowned. "I hoped we could hike."

"I walked all the way to Little Bear Lake."

Deedee went soft and sympathetic. "Okay, no big hike. I know the perfect place where we can go and just talk."

They took a tiny trail up the mountain a short way. Sitting on a huge boulder, they could see through the trees and into the valley. They settled in, back to back.

"I really don't know what to say to these kids when they ask me questions about God," Deedee said.

China snorted. "You know more than most people."

"Sure, I can give them information. But my own boredom doesn't make it very exciting."

"You worry too much. I've watched you with your girls. They adore you. They look up to you." China stopped and turned to face her friend. "Mine don't look up to me." She shook her head. "So what do you say to your girls when they ask?"

Deedee shrugged. She leaned back, her wild, curly hair falling behind. "I tell them that sometimes it really doesn't seem like God is there. Or that it doesn't work out quite the way the camp speakers sometimes make it sound. It isn't easy being a Christian." She blushed. "Other stuff like that. My dad would probably kill me if he found out."

China stared at her friend. "You tell them this?"

Deedee blushed. "You hate me, don't you?"

China shook her head. "No, and that's probably why the girls love you. You're real. You don't give them fake, happily-ever-after answers. What amazes me is that you're actually having these conversations with these kids. Mine don't listen to me. They're so busy running around and cutting up on people that they don't have time to listen. I bore them."

Deedee drew a strand of hair behind her ear. "You really think they *like* to hear things that aren't sweet answers?"

China nodded. "I, on the other hand, am failing miserably. All I wanted to do this week was make a difference in the life of one girl."

"What makes you think you're failing?"

"I know the girl has to be Irene. She's so . . . so . . ."

"Big?"

China laughed. "That, too. But nobody likes her. So I figured if I show her what it's like to have someone like her, then maybe I can make a difference in her life. She'll go on to become someone famous, and all because of one camp counselor who cared."

Deedee leaned forward, bent around to look at China, and shook her head. "You're hopeless," she said.

"What?"

"There you go with your wild imagination again."

China crossed her arms and frowned into the distance.

"First of all, who do you think you are that you can make a lifelong difference in someone's life? Second, you don't even like her."

China peered at Deedee. "Some friend you are." She recrossed her arms and pouted.

"China, I'm not trying to be mean. I'm saying that if our being counselors makes a difference in some girl's life—that's up to God, not us. It would be God's work, not ours. We just kind of stumble along doing dumb things."

"I thought God needed us."

"Not really."

"Why are there missionaries if He doesn't?"

"God doesn't really need us. He's big enough to do it all Himself. But He does use us when we're willing to let Him."

"Well, I'm willing, and I want Him to."

"Sometimes the best times are when we least expect them and aren't trying."

"Oh, and you have so much experience in life to tell me this." China propped her chin in her hands, her elbows on bent knees. She knew she shouldn't let her frustration fall out on Deedee.

Deedee grew quiet. After a long silence, she spoke. "It's only because I grew up here, okay? I hear lots and lots of people's stories about what changed their lives.

I know the speakers they're talking about. I've seen so many whose lives are touched by things we'd never expect—a waitress who smiles when she serves, the mountains standing tall and strong."

"And the words and teaching of the speakers never change their lives?"

"Sure they do. But even the speakers will tell stories of how, when they least expected it, God used them." Deedee reached for China's hand. "I just don't want you to work so hard for something you shouldn't be working for. Just be yourself."

"Oh, no. Myself is always getting in trouble."

Deedee laughed. "You never know what God can use."

China shook her head. "And here I thought I needed Magda around."

"See!" Deedee said, tipping her head way back to look at China upside down. "You certainly didn't expect to learn anything from me."

They sat then, saying nothing, hugging their knees. A warm afternoon breeze gently lifted their hair. The canyon below looked thick with trees. Beyond, Grizzly Creek cut a path through the forest, and the steady crash and tumble of the water soothed and comforted.

Just when China felt she might doze off, a crashing through the bushes grabbed her heart and shot fear through it. She reached for Deedee. Neither of them spoke. Both knew what the other was thinking: *Bear.*

## CHAPTER THIRTEEN

**T**HE "BEAR" CRASHED through the brush and trees as if it were running from or intent on chasing something. A funny noise made China cock her head. Then she loosened her grip on Deedee's arm. "I don't think it's a bear," Deedee whispered.

China nodded. "Bears don't mutter."

Both girls giggled softly.

"Idiot," came an angry male voice from up the trail. "She can rot for all I care. Barbie dolls. Pretty to look at, nice to hold. Plastic. That's all they are, plastic." The crashing stopped, and the voice sounded as though it had changed direction to shout up the hill, "You deserve your title!" Seconds later, a dark-haired, good-looking boys' counselor from the Tribal Village landed in their clearing. He didn't even look surprised to see two wide-eyed girls watching him.

"She can rot. I really mean that," he said without introduction. "Oh!" he said in a phony girl's voice. He wobbled around and fell. He threw the back of his hand to his forehead. "Oh!" he cried again. "I've hurt my *ankle*. I don't think I can *walk*. Can you carry me out, Michael?" He rubbed his ankle and stuck out his lower lip. He rolled his eyes up at the girls and batted his eyelashes.

Both of them immediately knew he was talking about Heather.

"Ice Queen is a good name for her. She lives up to that in many ways. I won't put up with it. She's a tease. A liar. A fake."

With that, he stomped off, still muttering under his breath.

Deedee raised her eyebrows. "Well, now, that was quite a show," she said.

Then they both burst out laughing.

"Do you really think she's hurt?" China asked.

Deedee shrugged her shoulders. "Hard to tell."

Both girls looked up the mountain. They kept quiet, waiting for an angry Heather to come marching through the brush. Deedee looked at her watch and suggested, "Let's give her 10 more minutes."

After 10 minutes, Heather still hadn't come. Deedee checked the time. "We have 20 minutes before we have to get back."

China looked up at the mountain and listened. She didn't hear anything. "Could she have gone back another way?"

"I suppose. But it isn't likely. If Mike was mad enough to just hike straight down the mountain . . ."

She screwed up her mouth, and her eyes narrowed.

"Do you think she's in trouble?"

"If she's up there on the mountain alone, with no trail nearby, she's in trouble."

"Doesn't she know the mountain real well? She keeps telling everyone she was raised up here."

"Heather? Hike? Be brave and explore? The only exploring Heather ever did was to see how her clothes fit and how they affected the male population."

"Do you think she needs help?"

"This is Heather we're talking about. We know she needs help. But whether or not *she* thinks she needs help is a different story."

China shuddered. "I sure hope she never becomes a brain surgeon. I'd hate to think of her in a job where help is vital but she thinks she never needs it."

Deedee shuddered, too. "I can't imagine Heather being any kind of doctor, except maybe a plastic surgeon. Then she could make everyone beautiful."

"And she could point to all the beautiful people and say she was responsible for them being that way."

"Too bad there aren't plastic surgeons for the heart. She could sure use one."

"Does she even have a heart? Is there anything about Heather that's good and nice and human?" China continued, "My girls and I were talking about loving someone who is unattractive and stupid. But how can we love someone who's gorgeous and mean? I think it was Snoopy in the Peanuts cartoon who said, 'Beauty is only skin deep, but ugly goes clear to the bone.'"

Deedee laughed. "He must have met Heather."

"Can *you* love Heather? You don't seem to have trouble loving or accepting anyone."

Deedee chewed on her cheek. Tears came to her eyes. "I used to love Heather. I loved her with all my heart. I thought we could be best friends. She was so full of life and laughter. She didn't like to do the fun outdoors stuff that I did, but she liked to have fun and talk. Little by little, though, she ripped off pieces of me as if it didn't matter. Do you know how many times she dumped me when we were younger? Only a couple years ago, she would promise to do something with me, and then the second a good-looking guy came along, or someone pretty like her, I was history and she was off flirting or laughing. I was always her friend until something better came along."

"I don't suppose we have any good reason to help her," China said. "She's never been nice to us."

Deedee shook her head.

"If we hadn't been here, we would never have known she was up there," China continued. "She would be left there anyway. So maybe it was meant to be."

"She thinks she knows everything about this camp," Deedee said. "Maybe it's time someone showed her how much she doesn't know."

"Her lies need to be exposed," China agreed.

Deedee slipped off the boulder, brushing the seat of her shorts.

"If we leave her there, what's the worst thing that could happen to her?" China asked.

"A bear could come along and eat her for dinner."

"We know that most bears are afraid of people. So unless she smells like food, that's not a problem." China smiled. "She smells more like a flower garden than anything else. Do bears like flowers?"

"Probably not to eat."

China slid from the boulder and stretched. "What else could happen?"

"She could get cold, hungry, scared . . ."

They looked at each other.

"I know that wouldn't really hurt her any," Deedee said. "Maybe teach her a good lesson."

China snapped her fingers as the light went on in her head. "That's it! I'll bet God wants to teach her a lesson. You even said that sometimes God teaches people in a way they would never expect. If we go up there, we'll be interfering with His lesson."

"Major good point." Deedee looked out into the canyon. "Every time we've tried to help her before, she only gets angrier and worse than before. It's like she resents us helping."

"Do you think she feels we're better than she is if we help?"

"She couldn't feel very good about it. Can you imagine if you thought you were Miss Perfection, yet the two dweebs you hate most in life are always coming to your rescue?"

China laughed. "That would be a little disheartening. So here are our choices," she continued, pacing back and forth, her hands behind her back. "If we help her, we could be interfering with God's plans."

Deedee nodded.

"Also if we help her, she's only going to get mad at us and be even meaner than before."

"Amen to that."

"If we don't help her, the worst thing that could happen is she would get a little cold, hungry, and scared."

"Right. And if we help her," Deedee said, "we'll never get any thanks."

"If we help her, she'll lie and tell everyone we were lost and she had to help us find our way back."

"So why should we help her?" Deedee asked tentatively. "Would she help us?"

"Not in a million years," China said firmly.

"Everything points to the fact that we shouldn't help her," Deedee said confidently.

"Right," China agreed. "Besides, we need to get back in just a few minutes to be with our kids."

They stood and looked at each other. They spoke without a word, making a joint decision without a sound. They hated the decision. They hated it beyond any of the dumb things they'd done and stupid decisions they had ever made. But they made it anyway and knew they would do it without looking back. Without regrets.

China sighed and shook her head. "Why do we always have to do what's right?" she said. "Why can't we ever just walk away and pretend we didn't know anything about it?"

"Probably because we care about what God wants more than anything."

"I heard Kemper say that God's way isn't the easy way—it's usually the most difficult—but it *is* the best way."

"We'd better get going then."

"You lead the way."

Deedee stood for a moment, her hands on her hips, her eyes scanning the mountain. "I suppose Mike took her up the Starlight Trail toward the peak. There's lots of pretty views and meadows up there."

"So why can't Heather just take the trail back?"

"If he came charging down the mountain, it's probably because they lost the trail. It's easy to get lured into a meadow or by the small rush of water from a waterfall. It's called Starlight Trail because it's easily lost. So many people end up watching the stars until they can find their way back the next day. It's not a recommended trail for Crazy Bear campers unless they've been coming here for years."

Deedee led China to the trail. "Even if Mike knew where the trail was, he probably figured Heather wouldn't follow him through the brush, where she'd get scratched up and her clothes dirty and ruined."

Deedee moved ahead, sure and quick. China

followed. She felt tired and wished she could be doing anything else, but she forced herself to go on. Ahead lay a long trail. At the end waited an ungrateful, crabby person with lots of mean things to say to them. *Just how I wanted to spend my afternoon,* China thought with a sigh.

# CHAPTER FOURTEEN

**B**ECAUSE OF THE RECENT RAIN, the ground was damp and cool. The sun filtering through the branches met with the moisture and made the air muggy and uncomfortable. The girls didn't say much on their way up the mountain. China could only think of how silly it seemed to be looking for a girl who hated her guts—a girl who certainly wouldn't bother to come to *her* rescue. She kept herself going by reminding herself this would look good on her spiritual résumé. It was the right thing to do.

The higher they went, the cooler it got and the sparser the trees grew. A number of times, Deedee stopped, looked around, and then moved on. Three times they left the main trail and traveled back into thick brush and trees. Each time they found an empty meadow, clearing, or brook. Once inside a little oasis, China realized how easy it might be to get lost. If she didn't pay attention to where they were going, she might not have realized what opening they had used to get in.

"How do you think we'll find her?" China asked.

Deedee didn't answer right away. She continued to move up the mountain, her arms pumping, helping her gain momentum when the trail grew steep.

"I can't imagine Heather willing to come up this far," China said.

"One thing for me to think about at a time," Deedee replied. She stopped and looked around again. "I think if we don't find her on the next few tries, we assume she went down another way. But I think you're right—I can't imagine Heather coming up this far unless a cute guy was paying attention to her."

The trail narrowed and veered to the left. Deedee went straight, as if she didn't even see the trail. The wet ground had some fallen leaves on it that looked as though they had been munched into the ground. "I'll bet she's here," Deedee said.

She moved easily through the trees into an empty clearing. "Heather?" she called. "Heather!" she called louder. She started walking the perimeter of the clearing, peering through the trees.

One end of the clearing sloped up. Over by some rocks that had slipped down the mountain, China pointed to a sandal lying on the ground. "Heather's."

"Look." Deedee showed China a mark in the damp ground made by what looked like someone sliding, then falling in the dirt. "If she's hurt, she's around here somewhere."

"Go away," said a petulant voice from behind a boulder.

They rolled their eyes at each other and walked over to the boulder. There Heather sat, mud on her leg and the side of her dress. With arms crossed and eyes blazing with fury, she repeated, "Go away."

"We thought you might need some help," China said.

"You thought wrong," Heather replied.

China wanted to throw the sandal at Heather and walk away. "Let her rot," Mike had said. China agreed.

"Michael will be back to get me."

China and Deedee exchanged glances again. "I don't think so," Deedee said kindly. "He's pretty mad."

"Oh, he *is*, is he? And what right does *he* have to be mad?" Heather searched their faces to see what reason he gave them.

"We don't really know," Deedee told her. "We only know he stomped off pretty furious. He said he was going to let you rot up here."

"Okay, I will. It'll serve him right. Then he'll be sorry."

"Will he?" Deedee asked pointedly.

Heather lost her look of anger. For a split moment, a profound sadness crossed her face. "Probably not," she admitted.

"So what do you want us to do?" Deedee asked.

"I said to go away and leave me alone."

"We need to get back to our campers. Are you going

to return soon? We'll need to let them know when you're coming."

Heather burst into tears. China and Deedee stared at her. "I don't *want* you to help me," she cried. "I don't want anyone to help me." She wiped the back of her hand across her face, leaving a black streak and miraculously stopping the flow of tears. "I'll be down when I'm good and ready to come."

The girls stood rooted to the spot. Neither said a word. Neither knew what to do. Neither felt they should leave.

"What're you staring at?" Heather hissed.

"Are you comfortable sitting there?" Deedee asked.

"It's none of your nosy business."

For the first time, China noticed Heather's knee and ankle. Both were swollen and turning purple. She hadn't seen them before because the nearer leg was fine, and the hurt leg was hidden in the shadows. "You can't hike down the trail," China said.

"I can too. I just don't want to." Heather crossed her arms and looked the other way.

"Prove it," Deedee said.

"I don't have to."

"We're not leaving until you do."

Heather stared at her. Deedee stared back.

"Fine," Heather spat. She placed her hands on each side of her legs and leaned forward. She bent her good leg and tried to push herself up with the help of the boulder behind her. She winced and cried out in pain.

"Ouch!" she said, looking at the palm of her hand. "I guess I put my hand on a thorn."

"Okay," Deedee said. "We'll go and leave you alone."

The girls wheeled around and left the clearing. Once out of earshot, Deedee said, "I'll go get help. We'll come back with a stretcher. You stay here and keep an eye on her."

"Why can't *I* go get help?" China asked.

"Could you find your way back to camp?"

"Probably."

"Then could you find your way back here again— maybe in the dark?"

China sighed. "No. But I'm not enjoying the thought of being alone with Heather, you know."

"Pretend you're not here."

"Huh?"

"Stay out of sight. Don't let her see you." Deedee untied her flannel shirt from around her waist. "Take this. She'll probably need it eventually."

China hated watching Deedee go down the hill and disappear. She wasn't scared of bears, mountain lions, bugs, or other wild animals. But she was scared of being alone with Heather. Doing the silent Indian walk, China skirted the clearing until she was within 20 yards or so of Heather. She found a dry patch and sat down to wait out the hours it might take for Dee- dee to return.

China started out sitting up against a tree. She closed her eyes and let her mind take over. She imagined

every step down the mountain, ticking off the minutes she was stuck here until Deedee returned. Her
head felt heavy, so she lay down on the ground, curl-
ing up in a little ball. The air moved over her, stroking
her cheeks and hair. It felt just like her baby-sitter's
fingers when she was small. Soon she fell asleep.

## CHAPTER FIFTEEN

"I HATE YOU, Michael Cochran!"

China bolted upright. Her mind, heavy with sleep, tried to decipher what she had heard.

"I swear I'm going to get you!"

China pulled a couple pine needles from her face. She sat up, trying to get her brain and limp muscles to catch up with the rest of her wakening body. *Well, that's no idle threat,* she thought. *Heather's methods of revenge can be devastating.*

An agonized cry of pain followed. Then sobs. "Oh, God, it hurts. I can't move. It's not fair."

China winced. She knew Heather was trying to stand.

"I hate them all!" Heather shouted to the mountain. "Michael, China, Deedee, Daddy, Momma! All of them!"

*Oh, great.* China's slumbering brain dredged up an old fact. *Heather's mom is dead. She hates her?*

Through a heavy outburst of tears, Heather called out, "And sometimes, God, I even hate You!"

135

China thought her heart had stopped. She cringed, waiting for the lightning to zip through the trees and incinerate the whole area. But nothing happened. God must have stepped away from the controls for a moment and missed that one.

Heather's crying continued. Sometimes her tears were punctuated with a cry of pain.

China put her face in her hands. "God, I can't take this," she prayed. "I can't sit here and listen to someone cry like that." Then she stood, trying to get up enough nerve to approach Heather. Suddenly a thought came to her: *What can she do to you? She can't get up and chase you. There aren't any sharp objects nearby for her to throw. The only thing she can hurt you with are her words. And you're used to that. Go for it. I'll be with you.*

China often wondered if thoughts like that were from her own brain or God. They seemed to talk differently than her own brain. And her own brain certainly wouldn't tell her to jump into the middle of a firing squad. China sighed and walked purposefully toward Heather.

Heather sat with her hurt leg in the same position as before. She had her head in her hands, sobbing.

"Heather," China said as kindly as she could, knowing her soft, susceptible insides were about to be attacked.

Heather looked up with bloodshot eyes, black speckles of makeup all over her face. She also needed a Kleenex for her nose. "I hate you," Heather said in a weepy voice. She dropped her head and cried some more.

China stared at Heather. All the prettiness had disappeared. Tears and pain had distorted all that made Heather striking and gorgeous. China forced herself to walk closer. She squatted next to Heather and touched her hair.

Heather squirmed away, then cried in pain again.

China stroked her hair again and smoothed back some strands from her face.

Heather squirmed again. She looked China in the eyes. "Don't you get it?" she said. "Are you stupid? I hate you. I *hate* you."

"I know," China said. "You're not my favorite person, either."

Heather looked at her, tears still pouring down her face. She cocked her head. "So why are you here?" she asked.

"We couldn't leave you—no matter how much we don't like you. I hid over there."

"You've been here all along?" Heather sounded angry and amazed at the same time. "Did you hear everything?"

"I don't know. I fell asleep. When you shouted just now, it woke me up."

Heather bent way over to wipe her drippy nose on her short dress. "You didn't hear much then."

China moved in front of her. "I can go if you want.

I'll go back there and wait until help comes."

"When is help coming?"

"Deedee figured it might be dark before they get here. They'll have to hike down to main camp after they make arrangements for all our girls. Then they have to get the rescue squad together. All of it takes time. So she said not to be scared. It will be dark, but they'll find us."

Heather thought about that. She seemed to be fighting a losing battle with anger. "You guys didn't leave me here," she muttered. "I can't believe you didn't just leave me here."

China waited.

"I . . . I guess you can sit."

"Do you need anything?"

"Water. I'm so thirsty."

China gave her a funny look. "I guess I shouldn't have asked if you need anything. I don't have anything to give you. Oh, wait." China ran back to her resting spot and returned with Deedee's flannel shirt. "Here. Deedee gave it to me in case you get cold."

Heather looked at it as if she'd never seen a flannel shirt.

"I know it's not your style, but you could use it as a pillow if you don't want to wear it."

Heather reached for the shirt. Her eyes welled with tears again. She put it on as if it were a fur coat. "Thanks," she said. "I really needed this."

China stared at her. Was this Heather? The Ice

Queen? Was she saying thanks, or was China hearing things? Maybe she was still asleep and dreaming all this.

China moved to one side so Heather didn't have to look at her. She hugged her knees and looked up at the dusky sky. It would get dark earlier here. And fast. A long time passed before Heather spoke again.

"Do you know why Michael left me here?" she asked pointedly. She wiped her face and looked at China.

China didn't know what to say. The Heather she knew didn't initiate conversation with the lowly China Jasmine Tate.

"Did he tell you anything?" Heather persisted.

*Ah, she just wants information to hang the guy with*, China thought. She looked at Heather, trying to decide if she should acknowledge what she knew.

Heather crossed her arms casually, an amused look on her speckled face. "Go ahead. It's okay. I won't bite." The tears had dried, the face returned to ice.

China moved to a position in front of Heather and bit her lip before she began to speak. "He said he wanted you to rot, that you were faking being hurt." China looked at the swollen, discolored leg. "I don't know how he could think that."

"*That's* what he told you? That's all?" Heather's voice was almost a shriek. China figured she'd be stomping around or flouncing if she weren't hurt. "That creep." Heather flung her arms out. "Did he tell you how I got hurt?"

China thought a moment, then shook her head. "No, he was too busy crashing through the forest. He made it sound like you did something to be dramatic and did a fake fall . . . in order to . . ." China blushed and couldn't go on.

"In order to what?" Heather tapped her long nails on her arm. "I'm waiting."

"In order to get his attention."

"Ha!" Heather shouted, fury steaming from her ears and shooting thousands of tiny darts from her eyes. "I got hurt running after him. I couldn't believe he'd actually leave me alone on the mountain—no matter *what* he thought." She looked at China to see if she caught her meaning.

"I could lie to you right now. I could," Heather continued hotly. "But what's the point? You probably won't believe me anyway. I've lied enough around you to never be believed again."

China's eyebrows went up. She'd thought Heather didn't have a clue that her lies had any effect on people except to make her look better.

"I'm going to tell you about what happened," Heather went on. "I figure you won't believe me, but who cares? I've got nothing to lose with you." She pulled her black hair away from her face, combing it with her nails. "I'll tell you so this never happens to you." She looked China over and frowned. "Not that it ever would."

China became instantly aware of her missionary-barrel clothes that didn't do a lot for her possible attractiveness to guys.

For Heather, it seemed China's frumpiness turned some sort of light on inside her, as if she suddenly saw something important. She seemed thoughtful for a moment, as if contemplating what the light showed her. She shook her head and said, "Like I said, I don't know if you'll believe me. Not that it matters anymore. Everyone will probably believe what Michael says. Why shouldn't they?"

China nodded, hoping Heather would continue.

"Michael kept being nice to me all week. I smiled at him, he smiled at me. We flirted. I flirt a lot. I admit it. I like it. It's fun most of the time. It was with Michael." Heather combed her hair again, smiling at the thought. A frown brought her back to the present.

"We talked about everything. His kids at camp. My kids. Families, school. You know, all the stuff you talk about with boyfriends."

China didn't really know. She didn't really care. She had great guy friends, and they talked about everything. She had only had one real boyfriend, and they never knew what to talk about. She nodded, however, because she wanted Heather to continue.

"So he asked if I wanted to go on a hike with him. He smiled until I melted into his eyes. Oh, yeah, I'd go. I'd go anywhere with that smile and those eyes. I gave him my best smile and my best eyes. Then he did this weird thing. He bit his lip and swallowed so hard I could see his Adam's apple slide up and down. He looked at the ground then up at me. 'It'll be okay,' he said. I looked at him funny and said, 'What?' He looked away quickly and muttered, 'I'm sorry. I was talking to myself.'"

China kept nodding, wondering at Heather talking with her like this. The only thing she could figure out was that Heather was so mad at Mike that her story was spilling out on the closest person, even if the closest person was someone she hated.

"So he gave my hand a squeeze, and we started hiking. I told him I wasn't really dressed for hiking, and he said it didn't matter. He wouldn't take me anywhere difficult."

She took a deep breath and continued. "The whole way up, I was slipping whenever we got into the mud. He took my hand and helped me through. A real gentleman. Then we got up here. We looked at the view, silent. What can you say in the face of such awesome mountains?"

China tried to keep her surprise from showing on her face. Heather awed by creation? This conversation was too much. She wrapped her arms around herself and pinched the tender skin on the back of her arm. Nothing changed. She wasn't dreaming.

Heather's face looked peaceful—maybe even with a touch of joy at the memory. She looked beyond China, seeing instead the beautiful afternoon. "We talked some about God. Michael put his arm around me." Heather sighed. "And then he pulled me to him . . ."

Heather stopped her story and looked at China. She studied her for a long time.

"He kissed you," China said.

"Yeah." Since China didn't fall over dead, start turning red, or come unglued, Heather continued. "His kiss was soft and sweet. I couldn't resist. I melted. Then, the kiss changed. It was more like he was trying to swallow me than be nice. Then he started . . . " Heather's voice trailed off, and tears formed in her eyes. Taking a deep breath, she said in a strong "who cares?" kind of voice, "Well, anyway, he started screaming at me."

China felt her brows pull together. This didn't make sense.

"'I can't believe this,' he yelled. 'I'm different now, do you hear me? I won't let you do this to me. I won't let you trick me into this. I've made a promise. I've got a ring. I'm going to wait for it all. I told God I wouldn't do this anymore now that I'm a Christian.'

"His face got all red. He looked like he was going to blow up into a thousand little bits like a balloon. And he said, 'It's all your fault.' He screamed again, running his hands through his hair. He stomped around like a mad man. 'You did this to me. It's you that's making me sin. You knew a kiss like that would make me want more. You know kissing me like that would make me want to touch you.'

"He walked away, muttering to himself, 'I can't

believe it. She did this on purpose. She's just lying. The conniving little wench.' Then he came back and got right in my face and yelled at me, 'You're a lying, conniving little wench! You know exactly what you're doing.'

"By then I was getting scared. He was acting real strange. I couldn't help it—I started to cry. For some reason, I cry easier when guys are around. Anyway, he started to stomp off and said over his shoulder, 'I won't let you seduce me! I won't!'"

China stared at her.

Heather nodded. "I stood there, looking like you. But I said, rather stupidly, 'What?'

"'You heard me,' he screamed. Then he repeated it.

"China, I swear I wasn't going to seduce him. I wouldn't. I really wouldn't. You've got to believe me. I may be a flirt and all, but I really don't want more than some sweet kissing. I mean, I do want more—I mean part of me does. But . . ." She stopped. She bit her lower lip and pressed her fist to her forehead. "I can't explain it. Part of me wants to do what is right, and part of me doesn't. But I've had a guy try something before, and he knew that was a mistake awfully fast. I only thought we were going to kiss a few times, then enjoy the view. How can I get Mike to believe that I wasn't trying to make him do anything?"

China had no answers. It's harder to prove you *weren't* going to do something.

Heather kept on, as though she really didn't expect

China to know how to solve her problem. "It was so weird, China. A few kisses and the guy thinks we're on the way to the whole thing. I don't get it. I felt nice, but nothing more. And here this guy thinks I'm leading him on. I really and truly don't get it."

China dug her finger into the moist dirt. She looked at the ground. "I'm sorry he misunderstood you, Heather." She didn't know what else to say. "Finish your story. How did you fall?"

"We were up there when all this happened." She pointed up a steep slope that probably had a gorgeous view from the rocks and trees. "He started to stomp down the mountainside. I started running after him. My sandals aren't the best for running in, and I slipped. My knee felt like it went one way and my ankle another. It was the final landing that I think did the most damage. He started running. I called after him and told him I'd hurt my leg. He didn't believe me. He just kept going." Heather paused and looked through the clearing as if he were just now disappearing from view.

"I kept calling," she continued, "but he kept going. I couldn't move my leg at all. I started scooting until I got here. But it hurt too much to go any farther. I figured I would just sit here until I found a way to hike down the mountain."

So Heather didn't really see herself as helpless.

"I hate him," she said. "How dare he think I'd try to get him to do something like that. How dare he leave me here! How dare he accuse me, call me names, and not even give me a chance to respond. He makes me sick."

It looked to China that Heather was *feeling* hurt more than anything.

Heather sighed. "So now that you know, do you hate him, too?"

China shook her head slowly. "I'm not happy about what he did," she said, "but I don't hate him."

"Why not?"

"Well, hate is such a *strong* feeling. I takes an awful lot for me to really hate someone."

Heather considered this and said, "I hate a lot of people."

"Why?"

"When they don't do what I want, it makes me mad."

"Why should everyone do what you want?"

"When you put it that way, the answer is obvious— they don't have to do what I want."

"So why do you hate them if they don't?"

Heather sat and thought. China figured she knew the answer but didn't know if she should tell it to one of her enemies. "Life is so scary," Heather breathed. "You never know what's going to happen. If you can make things happen your way, then you know you're in control and things will be okay. But when you're not in control . . . " Even in the near darkness, China could see Heather shudder.

"You can't always be in control," China suggested.

"I know. It's getting harder and harder. It's worth the try, though. If I can control, I can't be hurt. You'd think it would get easier as you get older. More power and choices and all. But it's not."

"I know. The older I get, the more everything else seems to be in charge of my life. You can't go around hating people all your life, Heather."

The veil came down over Heather's face. Once again she was the Ice Queen. China shivered at the chill in the air.

# CHAPTER SIXTEEN

**H**EATHER CLOSED HER EYES, but that didn't stop the tears from escaping. She tried desperately to hold on to the Ice Queen image—something no one could touch. Hard. Cold. In perfect control of everyone and everything. But the Ice Queen sat, still and tall, trying not to melt right before China's eyes.

China felt as if she were peeking in someone's window at night. But if she turned away now, she would never believe this could happen—that it was possible for the Ice Queen to become a real person. It already seemed like an odd dream. China wondered if she would wake in her cot in Rock tepee as the drum sounded three beats, and the Ice Queen and her dream would melt away into nothingness.

Heather sighed. "I guess you haven't found out yet," she said. "It's easier to hate people than to love them. Then when they leave or die, it doesn't hurt. It feels good."

China didn't know what to say. She sat like a good

148

little girl in church—her hands folded in her lap.

"I hate you," Heather said softly. "I really do."

China couldn't respond to that. It sounded more like a plea than a statement.

"I've always hated you."

"I've always wondered why," China finally said, her voice reflecting Heather's.

"You—" Heather's tears took over for a moment, flooding her face. After a few sobs, her enormous self-control took over. "You have friends."

"So do you," China said. "You have more than anyone I've ever seen."

"You have friends because they like you. I have people who hang around me, but they aren't really my friends."

China thought about that.

"All my life I've wanted to have a true friend. Someone who likes me for who I am, not for what I look like or for how much money I have."

China felt totally confused. She was afraid to say anything. Heather's vicious venom felt too fresh for China to pop words out of her mouth the way she did with Deedee. First she ran the words over in her mind and selected the tone of voice she would use. "Then why do you push how you look?" she asked. When Heather didn't attack, China went on. "You always dress in ways that make you look positively gorgeous. It's as if you're trying to attract people like a flower attracts bees."

Heather nodded. China felt herself get real brave—or real stupid. She wasn't sure which. "How can someone like you for who you are when you are so mean to people?"

"I guess I'm hoping they'll keep trying to break through the wall of protection I've put up." Heather sighed. "Nobody tries to knock the wall down. They just sit back and admire it. I'm just a *thing* to people, China."

China figured she was in the middle of a dream or going into shock. No. She had to be dying. Heather wouldn't be telling her all this stuff if China wasn't about to die. Heather probably planned to push her off the mountain. *Oh, well*, she thought. *Here goes nothing*.

"No one likes to be attacked over and over, Heather," she said. "Why should I try to be friends with someone who hates me? I'm not about to form a friendship with someone who enjoys seeing me bruised and bloody."

"I know. I know."

It suddenly seemed to get darker. China shivered. Still, she had to ask. "Heather, do you really hate God?"

Heather looked off into the trees, peering into the beginnings of a starry night, her face cold and thinking. Then she turned her icy gaze to China. As her eyes searched every inch of China's face, China felt exposed. She almost wrapped her arms around herself to protect her innermost self from Heather's thorough search.

Whatever Heather saw must have made it all right for her to speak. She still took her time about it. She combed her hair back with her nails. She tried to shift and winced in pain. She clasped her perfect hands around one bent knee. "Yes," she said, her answer more like a puff of escaped air.

"Why?" China asked in the same soft breath.

"I don't think it's fair that He's supposed to be in control of everything, and then He takes things away from people. He won't stop bad stuff from happening."

"What kind of bad stuff?" China asked softly, as if using her real voice would keep this new Heather from talking.

"I want my mom," Heather whispered. "I want her so bad sometimes. It hurts inside in a way that makes me ache. I want her back. It's not fair." Heather's voice grew louder and louder. "It's not fair! *It's not fair!*"

China felt herself grow red. She had gladly left her own family for the summer. She didn't miss her mom much—didn't miss anyone. And here was Heather, wanting a mom desperately.

"God scares me," Heather went on. "He wants me to give Him control of my life. But when I do, bad things happen. People love you. Then they leave. They get close to your heart, get you to finally trust again, and then they drop you. Leave. Take another slice of your heart when they go."

Suddenly China felt so sheltered. Everyone she ever loved was still there somewhere—maybe far away, but still connected. Her heart felt whole.

"I hate God. I hate Him for not keeping my mother alive. I hate Him for allowing my dad to date and then never finalize a relationship with any of those women. I hate Him for asking me to pledge my total allegiance to Him when I can't. I can't trust Him with anything small, so how can I trust Him with something as big as my life?"

"But God is your father," China protested. "And your father is loving and provides for you and wants the best for you."

If looks could kill, China would have breathed her last. "My father sends me away whenever possible," Heather said in a hard voice. "My father says I'm ugly and stupid and I'll never be as good as him. My father provides for me, all right. He gives me a wad of money and never says a word about what I buy. Sometimes I wear these stupid clothes just to get some kind of response out of him. But I get nothing. My dad is too into himself to really care about me. Do I want that kind of God? Is that what God is about? If it is, then I really want nothing to do with Him."

China was speechless. She'd never thought about God as anything but a great father. Well, that wasn't really true. She often wondered if God had more important things to tend to than worry about a girl named China.

"My father knows I hate dirt. He hates dirt as much as I do. But he sends me to the Tribal Village to counsel. Not only that, I'll bet he made sure you and I were together as a cruel trick. He hates you as much as I do. He would think it pretty funny to put two fighting cats together to see what happens. He would call it a lesson. I think he's just being mean. He also knows I hate little kids. I can't relate to them. I can't deal with the constant bathroom humor, jokes about passing gas, and burp contests. Their petty fights over who said what to whom make me crazy. My dad knows this and puts me with a whole tepee of them in the middle of the dirt."

"You've done okay," China said, trying to be encouraging.

"Oh, yeah, right. I fall apart and run away when you guys need me the most. I teach them to be snobs. I care more about guys than I do about them. Quit lying, China. It doesn't become you."

China felt put back into the place of an underling, a stupid slum child who didn't know any etiquette. She wished she had something to say, something that would help Heather understand and believe that God loves her. "Yeah," she said, feeling stupid for even talking. "It's scary to let God be in control." China remembered the frightening flight from Guatemala and the terrifying prospect of spending the summer with Aunt Liddy. "But sometimes He makes surprising good things happen out of stuff that looks bad at the beginning. He says that all things work together for good."

"Don't quote that stuff at me. Nothing good came out of my mother's death. Nothing good came out of either week I spent with you at camp. At high school camp, I lost all my friends. This one has gone wrong from the beginning." Heather crossed her arms and turned her head. China could see tears starting to drip from the corners of her eyes again.

"Hello!" came a voice from the dark. "China! Heather! Are you there?"

"We're here!" China called.

Off in the distance, small beams of light ricocheted off trees. China jumped up and threw her arms around Heather. She hugged her tight. "You're not so bad, Heather Hamilton," she said firmly. "God will take care of you. You wait and see."

The rigid Queen of Ice began to melt and almost snuggle like a lost child into China's hug. At the sound of footsteps and people talking, however, she turned rigid again. China backed off quickly, knowing Heather would not want people to see her melt.

"How can you know, China?" Heather asked quickly, her eyes darting toward the approaching sounds. "How can you know God will take care of me? He hasn't done such a great job of it yet."

China's mind raced for an answer, one that would be true but not a false promise. "Think about tonight," she said. "You got hurt, and God sent me and Deedee to find you. He didn't leave you alone during the long hours you had to wait. Now the rescue people are here. Maybe life is like that. Maybe you just have to hold on, even though you're in great pain for a long time in the dark, until the rescue finally comes. Maybe God won't seem like He's coming through for years and years. Maybe it'll happen sooner—I don't know. Just don't give up on Him. Like Chief Black Bear said, God is much bigger and greater than we can ever imagine."

Heather leaned forward as far as she could. She reached out her hand and patted China on the leg. Seconds later, they were bathed in circles of light. The rescue crew checked Heather's leg against her protests that she didn't want anyone touching her until she saw their credentials. "What took you so long?" she demanded. "You leave me with the person I hate most in this world for what? So you could eat dinner first? Didn't you even think we might be hungry?"

For the first time, China realized she was very, very hungry.

"Oh," Deedee said, "I almost forgot." She reached into a small backpack and produced a couple of sandwiches. She gave one to Heather and one to China.

Deedee gave China a hug. "I can't believe you're sitting here with her," she whispered quickly into China's ear. "She didn't kill you?"

China looked at Heather, whose dark eyes pleaded

with her. She looked at Deedee and shook her head.

"Get me out of here," Heather demanded. She glared in China's direction. "I've spent way too much time here with people I can't stand."

The rescuers covered her with a blanket and strapped her onto a stretcher. As they moved away, a barrage of verbal abuse erupted from Heather's mouth.

Deedee gave China a sweatshirt, which China pulled over her head. "Thanks," China said.

"So tell me, tell me," Deedee said. "I'm dying to know how it went. I felt so bad leaving you here with her. I knew it was the best thing logistically. But I was still worried."

China moved toward the trail. She felt tired to the very core. Visions of Heather came to mind—her face so full of emotional pain, her words from a hidden place inside her. China shook her head. "I don't want to talk about it," she said. She didn't feel she could.

"That bad, huh?" Deedee said. China felt the spell of the melting Ice Queen would be broken if she said anything. She felt it would be yet another betrayal for Heather. And she felt as though nothing she could say would be fair.

They walked silently down the mountain, Deedee in front, her flashlight showing the way. China followed, alone with her thoughts.

# CHAPTER SEVENTEEN

I T SEEMED TO CHINA that she had been gone forever from her tepee. Singing Bird had helped Sky tepee's girls move their gear into Rock tepee. Now it was crowded with cots, girls, and luggage. The girls China had been so frustrated with now seemed like her own. Each face represented something special to her. Even Irene's.

Irene's cot still seemed a little isolated from the rest, but it wasn't quite so obvious as on the first day.

"You creep!" Mashiek shouted. "You just crunched my jewelry box I was going to give my mom!"

"It's only made out of stupid Popsicle sticks!" Li shouted back.

Mashiek crouched over her smashed box and said, "But it had pretty jewels all over it."

China helped pick up the pieces. "I think it can be glued back together," she said. "I don't think any of the sticks are broken."

A moment later, Laura asked, "What game are we

playing tomorrow, China?"

"I don't know. I missed the meeting."

"I sure hope Heather won't be coming back," Rhonda said. "I like you better."

China finally got the girls settled into their cots, read the evening's Scripture, and got them talking softly about the week. She asked them to discuss the most important thing that had happened to them at camp.

"I'll be first," Mashiek said, waving her hand wildly from her cot. "I learned that being pretty inside is more important than being pretty outside."

Li went next. "God is so huge. I think I'll probably never make Him tiny by thinking He can't do something again."

"I learned never to drink a glass of punch without looking for bees first," said a small girl with a swollen lip.

"I discovered that you have to look at a cute guy, then look away when he looks at you, kind of smiling when you do it," said one of Heather's girls. A few pillows flew across the tepee and hit her squarely on her head and body.

"And I learned that everyone has a special place in God's heart, even if they're way different from me," Lana said, looking at Irene. The other girls in the tepee nodded.

Irene shrugged her shoulders when China called on her. "I don't know," she said. "Nothing special, I guess."

A flush of sadness filled China—sadness that all she had hoped for hadn't happened. These girls learned about God. Some grew, some made decisions, and some stayed on the same level at which they arrived. Most had even come to accept Irene. But not one had experienced a lifelong change because China had been there.

China laid her head on her pillow and looked up toward the poles connected with leather ties. Their support meant the tepee wouldn't fall in. She thought over the past several days, letting the girls' bedtime chatter drift by unnoticed. She fell asleep thinking she could have been in Guatemala for all the help she'd been that week.

In the morning, Heather arrived just in time for the games. China couldn't believe her eyes. Heather? Back? She had an ankle-to-thigh brace, and she perched on a pair of wobbly crutches. She flirted mercilessly with all the guys, pointedly ignoring Mike. He seemed embarrassed at her brace, now knowing he really had been a jerk to leave her on the mountain.

China didn't know what to say or how to act. Should she be nice to Heather? Pretend they were old friends? She didn't know how the previous night had affected things between them. She cautiously stepped up to Heather and said, "I hope you're okay."

Heather stuck her nose in the air. "Okay enough," she sniffed.

"Your girls are in my tepee so they'd have someone to be with."

Heather sneered. "Are you trying to take my girls away?"

China shook her head. "You can have them back if you're staying."

"I'm staying. I want them back." Heather hitched her way over to her girls and called them all into a circle.

China felt slapped in the face. She also felt weird, as if the night before had never happened. *Maybe Heather opened a small window into herself and is now embarrassed, so she slammed it shut,* China figured.

That afternoon, as Deedee and China spent their free time together, Deedee said, "Are you going to tell me about it now?"

"About what?" China asked.

"About what happened last night."

China stared at the ground as they walked. "Nothing happened last night."

"You can't lie."

"I'm not lying."

Deedee studied her friend. "Something happened. All day, Heather's been watching you out of the corner of her eye. She doesn't hate you anymore."

"She does too. Didn't you hear her last night?"

"No. Those were fake words. She didn't mean it."

China shook her head. She was so confused. She didn't know what to think.

"Okay, we'll change the subject," Deedee offered.

"Please do," China said.

"I don't understand it," Deedee said. "My girls seem to have a deeper faith in God. It's very weird. I tell them I don't have the answers, that if I could really understand God, that would make Him so small that He wouldn't really be God anymore. So it can be good that we don't understand Him. And I tell them to look at the verses in the context of all the other verses around them so they don't misread what they're meant to say."

China was glad to have something to take her mind off the mystery of Heather. "See?" she told Deedee. "You do have something to give these kids."

"Like what? I tell them all this stuff that doesn't give them nice, easy answers, and I'm watching them grow. It doesn't make sense."

"Deeds, you give people something solid to hang on to. Sometimes Christian speakers want everyone to think being a Christian is something easy and wonderful—kind of like Christmas every day. When they find out it's not like that, they leave God in the dust and go on to something that appears to be more solid."

"That's always been my complaint about the speakers," Deedee said. "I've tried their ways, and sometimes they don't work. Sometimes they do. I think God just wants us to trust Him no matter how bizarre or painful things look on the surface."

"And so what you're giving your girls is a lesson in trusting, even though everything around them says not to trust—that things are falling apart. You're telling them the Great God, as Chief says, is much bigger than they can imagine. What better thing is there than that?"

A warm smile, coming from the deep inner part of her, warmed Deedee's face. China felt jealous. She could see Deedee felt good about herself as a counselor and about her week. It didn't seem fair. Her best friend had an answer to a prayer she hadn't even prayed. And China prayed and prayed and got no answer.

China spent the rest of the time with Deedee in some far-off land. She wasn't thinking much about anything, just drifting. She figured her brain was working overtime behind the scenes—working so hard that the front part of her mind couldn't think at all.

"Well, this was a fun afternoon," Deedee said at the end. "I'm glad we spent the time together."

"I'm sorry, Deedee," China said.

Deedee shook her head. "I wish I had been there last night. Something happened."

That evening, China kissed all her girls good night on the top of their heads. She gave them each a small gift of a bookmark for their Bibles and a candy bar they promised not to open until the next day. Then she slipped into bed with a sigh.

The next morning was a flurry of packing and good-byes. The girls all cried a little—all except Irene. China had to help her pack and roll her sleeping bag. Then all the girls enlisted China to roll their sleeping bags. "I can't do it," each girl pleaded, a big, sad look on her face. China gave in, wanting to do one last thing for the campers she had failed.

Laughing Squirrel came around, other Indians trailing behind him. Many of them wore beaded necklaces, moccasins, and headbands with feathers sticking out of them. All the Indians were a shade or two redder or darker from their hours in the sun. And all looked incredibly dirty. China ushered her kids out to Laughing Squirrel and returned to the silent, empty tepee to pack her own things and wait for Deedee.

*Crunch. Shuffle. Crunch. Shuffle.* China wondered where Heather was headed. A hand appeared at the door of the tepee. "Here," Heather said. An envelope dropped to the floor. Then Heather was gone. Smoking Buffalo, the food truck, stopped at the edge of their tribe. China heard Heather's flirtatious voice and the door creak open. She peeked out the tent opening in time to see an eager guy helping Heather into the truck. He threw her gear into the back and drove off.

China picked up the envelope. The words SLUM CHILD were printed in bold letters. China's hand shook as she opened it. She read each word. When she came to the end, she didn't think she understood or had read any of it. So she read it again.

Deedee appeared at the door. "Ready?" she asked.

China's hand shook as she held the letter out to Deedee. She couldn't say "Read this." She couldn't say anything.

Deedee held the letter and began to read out loud.

*Dear Slum Child*, it began.

"Oh, this is from Heather. How sweet," Deedee said sarcastically.

China waved at Deedee to keep reading, then started pacing, chewing on the edge of her finger, her tears close to the surface.

*I didn't expect the other night to happen. I didn't expect what came out of it. I can't really talk to you because I'm afraid I'll fall apart. I finally told someone my deepest secrets. There is so much you could do to hurt me now. I swore. I vowed. I knew I would never tell anyone what I felt again. But I've told you. And that's even scarier than crossing over a landslide in the middle of a thunderstorm.*

*When I told you, I was hurting. I would never have told you if I wasn't hurting. And scared. I still don't know why I told you anything. But when I did, I got the biggest surprise. You didn't make fun of me. You didn't laugh at me. You didn't even tell me I couldn't possibly be a Christian. You stayed. You listened. And as bad as I've treated you, you still cared.*

*I am going home today a different person. And it's all your fault. I'm going to start hoping that somewhere, somehow, God can take all this mess and do something with it. I'm going to start hoping that maybe God is a good father. I'm going to, for sure, go home with the hope that maybe I've finally found a real friend. You.*

*I hate to admit this, China. (It's so hard to say your name without screaming!) But you've changed my life. Maybe you don't care. Maybe you'll laugh hysterically when you read this letter. But it's true. If you tell anyone this, I'll tell them you're lying. I still have a reputation to keep. Besides, I don't know that I can change overnight. I don't know that I really want to give up control of my life. But in the dark, in the quiet of my heart, you will be my secret friend.*

*The hardest thing to say is that I hope you can forgive me. I've been very mean to you. And probably still will be in the light of day. But if you can forgive me, and maybe call me sometimes, I will try to learn how a friend should treat a friend.*

*Thank you, China. I will always be grateful.*

China sat on the floor and put her head in her hands. Deedee folded the letter and replaced it in the envelope. "What happened up there?" she asked for the zillionth time.

"You wouldn't believe it if I told you," China said. "I don't believe it, and I was there." China felt as if her voice came from outside herself.

Deedee's laughter started out slow, then moved higher and gained speed. She started laughing so hard she could barely stand it.

"What's so funny?" China asked.

After she had calmed down a little, Deedee managed to say, "Didn't you pray that God would help you change the life of just one girl this week?"

"Yeah," China said sadly. "And it didn't happen."

"Yes, it did. Yes, it *did!* Only you changed the life of the wrong person."

A smile started on one side of China's face and spread to the other. She started to shake her head. "I think God likes to do this," she said. "I think He gets a kick out of it. He answers our prayers, but sometimes in ways we would never imagine."

China took the letter and put it in her Bible. She prayed a quick, silent prayer. *God, Your sense of humor is intolerable.* She smiled. *Thanks for answering my prayer. Never in my wildest dreams would I have thought this could happen.*

China tucked her Bible into her duffel, then hoisted it onto her back and picked up her sleeping bag. "Come on, Deedee," she said. "Let's go home."

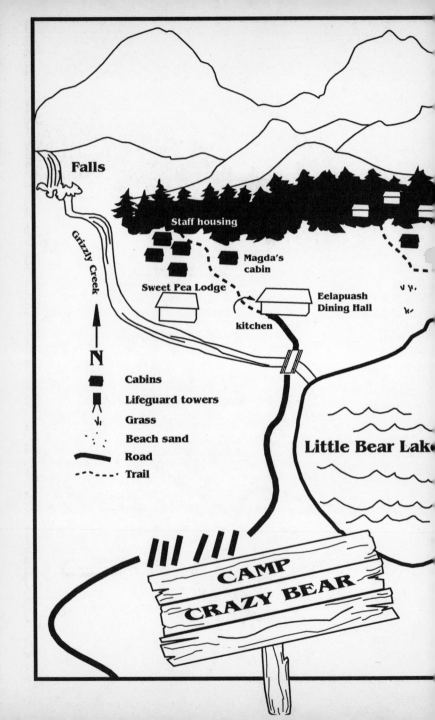

## DON'T MISS CHINA'S FIRST FIVE UNFORGETTABLE ADVENTURES!

*There's more action and excitement as China adjusts to life at Camp Crazy Bear. Although she's enjoying her independence, China finds that getting herself into trouble is easier than learning the biblical truths God wants to teach her.*

### SLICED HEATHER ON TOAST (#1)

*Heather Hamilton, the snobby camp queen, has it in for China from the moment they meet. It soon turns into a week-long war of practical jokes, hurt feelings and valuable lessons.*

### THE SECRET IN THE KITCHEN (#2)

*After becoming an employee of Camp Crazy Bear, China and her friend, Deedee, adopt a stray, deaf dog . . . even though it's against camp rules. Meanwhile, someone's planning a devious scheme that could cause great danger to China!*

### PROJECT BLACK BEAR (#3)

*Thinking it would be fun to have live bears for pets, China and Deedee set out food in an effort to lure the animals into camp. But these are wild California black bears, and the girls' good intentions have disastrous results.*

**WISHING UPON A STAR (#4)**
*When China discovers that the new kid in camp
is actually Johnny Foster of the hit TV show
"Family Squabbles," she dreams of a glamorous
Hollywood lifestyle—at the expense of her
friendship with Deedee!*

**A COMEDY OF ERRORS (#5)**
*China and Deedee overhear a terrible plot
to murder another camper. The two over-
imaginative girls don't realize that the
"murderers" are actually fiction writers.
Attempting to be heroes, the girls learn a
valuable lesson about eavesdropping and
jumping to conclusions.*

*Available at your favorite Christian bookstore.*